Hist
by)

MW00416129

Nvengaria series
(historical fantasy)
PENELOPE AND PRINCE CHARMING
THE MAD, BAD DUKE
HIGHLANDER EVER AFTER
THE LONGEST NIGHT

The Mackenzies
(Scottish Historical)
THE MADNESS OF LORD IAN MACKENZIE
LADY ISABELLA'S SCANDALOUS MARRIAGE
THE MANY SINS OF LORD CAMERON
THE DUKE'S PERFECT WIFE
A MACKENZIE FAMILY CHRISTMAS:
THE PERFECT GIFT
THE SEDUCTION OF ELLIOT MCBRIDE
THE UNTAMED MACKENZIE
THE WICKED DEEDS OF DANIEL MACKENZIE
SCANDAL AND THE DUCHESS
RULES FOR A PROPER GOVERNESS
THE STOLEN MACKENZIE BRIDE
A MACKENZIE CLAN GATHERING
ALEC MACKENZIE'S ART OF SEDUCTION
THE DEVILISH LORD WILL

Regency Pirates
THE PIRATE NEXT DOOR
THE PIRATE HUNTER
THE CARE AND FEEDING OF PIRATES

The Longest Night

Jennifer Ashley

Nvengaria
Book 4

Chapter One

December 1821

"YOU WILL SORT IT OUT, AUNT MARY, won't you? *Please?*"

Seventeen-year-old Julia Lincolnbury bleated this plea while she pirouetted in front of her dressing table. Mary looked up distractedly from where she folded underclothing, trying to make sense of the chaos of Julia's bedchamber.

Julia expected "Aunt" Mary Cameron to sort out everything in her life—her bonnets, her gowns, her invitations, her maids, and her mind. If Mary had been the young woman's governess or even her true aunt, she might feel obligated to do so, but Mary had offered to chaperone Julia solely as a favor to the girl's father.

Two weeks ago, when Mary had arrived in London to spend Christmas with her son, she'd happened upon Julia's father, a sad baronet called Sir John Lincolnbury, outside a bookshop on a gray

London street.

"Stuck in London for the winter," he'd said mournfully. His northern accent pronounced it *Loondon*. "I like th' quiet, but Julia is driving me mad. She made her bow in the spring, but no one's offered for her, poor gel. She's been invited to a Christmas ball at the Hartwells', the best invitation in Town, but of course she can't attend unchaperoned. If her poor, dear mother had lived …"

Julia's poor, dear mother had been Mary's closest childhood friend. When she'd died, Sir John had worked through his grief by spoiling Julia rotten.

"You *are* allowed to escort her to a ball, Sir John," Mary had pointed out as cold wind whipped at her skirts and oozed through her gloves. "You are her father, after all."

Sir John looked sadder still. "But a gel needs a wooman's hand, don't she? I can do nowt with her. And here we are in the south at an unfashionable time of year." Sir John eyed Mary in sudden hope. "I say, Mrs. Cameron, if you're stuck here like a lump as well …" He pronounced it *loomp*.

Mary had cut off what was certain to be a long, rather wet appeal to her charitable instincts. She had come to London early to wait for her son Dougal, who would journey here to begin his holidays from Cambridge. She'd decided to meet Dougal in London because back in Scotland, Castle MacDonald—her home—was preparing for another warm, happy, overflowing celebration, which only reminded Mary of her acute loneliness. This year her brother and his new wife celebrated the coming of their son, which made Mary, though she was deliriously happy for them, lonelier still.

"I'd be happy to chaperone Julia," Mary said

quickly. "For Allison's sake."

Sir John had brightened immeasurably, which meant that the lines of perpetual gloom on his face smoothed out a bit. "Splendid, Mrs. Cameron. This will cheer up Julia no end. She's moped about all through the shooting season in the north, and no amount of gowns and gewgaws will make her smile. Oh, you've changed me to a happy man indeed."

Mary had, the next morning, arrived at Sir John's home. Julia had gone into transports of joy that Aunt Mary would move into their London house and go with them to the Hartwell ball. Mary had received an invitation, as she had some acquaintance with the family, which made Mary, in Julia's eyes, second only to a goddess.

By the nineteenth of December, the day of the ball, Mary was reflecting that even her dear friend Allison wouldn't have asked her to take on such an onerous task as looking after Julia. But it was a distraction, and Mary needed distractions these days.

Julia held a new gown of pale yellow muslin against her body as she admired herself in the dressing table's mirror. "Lord Sheffley is certain to be at the ball. We must think of ways to keep him from dancing with that horrid Miss Hamilton. Aunt Mary, do think of something clever."

"The best way to attract a gentleman is to do nothing," Mary said as she untangled Julia's pile of ribbons. "If Lord Sheffley dances with Miss Hamilton, you pretend you don't care one whit for it."

"But I *do* care," Julia said, her jaw hardening. She gave the dress a wild swing. "I want to scratch her eyes out."

"You'll do nothing of the sort." Just as with Julia's

father, Mary had discovered that a firm tone worked wonders. "Remember what I said about manners."

Julia held on to her rebellious look, then under Mary's stare, wilted. "Yes, Aunt Mary," she said meekly.

Mary hid a sigh. Julia was naïve and feckless, but she meant well. Sir John had indulged her far too much, turning the sweet child Mary remembered into the unthinking, rather selfish creature she beheld now.

A bell rang downstairs. Julia dropped the yellow gown, which crumpled to the floor, and dashed out of the room. "The post has come!" she shouted at the top of her voice.

Mary bit back yet another exasperated sigh, picked up the dress, smoothed it out, and handed it to the lady's maid, who'd jumped up from her mending. Mary gave the poor, overworked young woman a little smile of sympathy and left the chamber in Julia's wake.

She reached the landing in time to see Julia, in the hall below, snatch a handful of letters out of the footman's gloved fingers. Julia sorted through them, dropping several and squealing when she found ones addressed to her.

"So much correspondence one has when one's friends are away in the country," she said as the long-suffering footman gathered the letters she'd dropped. "Oh, here's one for you Aunt Mary." Julia tossed it carelessly at Mary as Mary stepped off the last stair.

Mary took the letter, broke the wax seal stamped with the crest of Viscount Stoke, and opened it. The missive was from Lady Stoke, with whom Mary had made acquaintance when she'd come to London last spring. It was whispered that Viscount Stoke had once been a pirate, and Mary admitted that with his tanned skin, sundrenched hair, and shrewd blue eyes, he looked the part.

I was pleased to learn that you would be attending Lady Hartwell's ball tomorrow evening, Lady Stoke wrote. *It might interest you to know that the ambassador from Nvengaria and his wife will be there as well. Having met your brother, Mr. MacDonald, in Nvengaria, they are eager to make your acquaintance. The ambassador's aide, one Baron Valentin, indicated that he previously met you at your family's house in Scotland; indeed, that he stayed with your family for a number of months. I am certain you will enjoy this unlooked-for reunion.*

Mary's fingers went numb and the letter fell to the floor.

"Aunt Mary?" Julia asked, her jubilation turning quickly to concern. "Is it bad news? Your son?"

"No, no." Mary retrieved the letter before Julia could pounce on it. She held the paper away from the eager girl and crumpled it in her fist. "Not bad news. But I will not be able to attend the Hartwell Ball."

Mary turned and marched up the steps to her chamber, her heart hammering until she was sick with it, ignoring Julia's shrieks of dismay.

* * *

THE MAN NEEDED TO BE WATCHED.

Baron Valentin glided after the Nvengarian ambassador and his wife as they entered Hartwell House the night of the Christmas ball.

The house overflowed with ladies in glittering jewels, gentlemen in dark finery, the women in gowns of all colors of the rainbow. Garlands of greenery lined the windows, the friezes around the tops of the walls, and staircase banisters. Balls of mistletoe dangled from every doorway and chandelier.

The English had a bizarre custom—if a person paused beneath a clump of mistletoe, it was an invitation to be kissed. In Nvengaria, the parasitic mistletoe was a symbol of death, used in funeral wreaths. But Valentin had learned during his previous visit to the British Isles just how odd the Britons could be.

He had no interest in attending balls, even in one of the most lavish houses in London. Crowds unnerved him, English chatter unnerved him, and acres of bared female shoulders were unsettling.

But Valentin couldn't afford to let Duke Rudolfo out of his sight. Much as he chafed at this assignment, Valentin was not about to fail.

He walked a pace and a half behind Rudolfo, watching the much-ribboned hem of Duchess Wilhelmina's dress flow across the marble tiles. If the Hartwells' servants hadn't dusted the floor earlier it would be well dusted now.

Rudolfo led them into the ballroom, a lavish chamber with a mosaic-patterned ceiling that spoke of Near Eastern luxury. Lines of colorful ladies and monochromatic gentlemen met and parted in an English country dance, the room seeming to move.

Valentin couldn't help glancing through the throng, searching, seeking. He did not really expect to see the red-lipped, dark-haired Scottish lady he'd met last year, though he'd fallen into the habit of looking for her everywhere. She'd tended him when he'd been hurt, and her lilting voice had twined around his heart and pulled him back to life.

She wasn't here. Of course she wasn't. Mary would be in Scotland at her brother's castle, preparing for Christmas and Hogmanay. She'd be helping the housekeeper stir the black bun, perspiring in the warm kitchen while firelight glistened on her hair. She'd smile her rare smile that had made his blood sing.

Valentin had kissed her, touched her, asked her to come to him in Nvengaria. He'd gone home and waited for her through a brief, golden summer and a colder than usual autumn.

She'd never come. As the weather worsened, so did Valentin's hopes of opening the door of his rundown manor house to find Mary Cameron smiling on his threshold.

Why should she bother? The journey to Nvengaria, a tiny country wedged between the Austrian Empire and the Ottoman one, was long and dangerous, and Mary had every reason to stay in her brother's castle. Her new sister-in-law was having a baby, and Mary had a son of her own to look after, even if he was seventeen.

As an added complication, Valentin was part logosh, one of the strange and magical creatures that inhabited Nvengaria's mountains. Mary knew that. She'd seen him shift to his animal form—a black wolf—and she'd not been upset by it. Perhaps after Valentin had departed for Nvengaria, she'd had second thoughts about promising herself to a man who was part animal. That fact would make even Nvengarian women think twice.

Valentin had resigned himself to the fact that Mary wasn't coming. That he'd likely never see her again unless he sought her out.

When Grand Duke Alexander had come to Valentin and asked him to journey to England to keep an eye on Duke Rudolfo, Valentin had quickly agreed. He'd already decided to make his way to Scotland again and find Mary—to know—and had seized on the opportunity to travel this far.

Ambassador Rudolfo *didn't* know Valentin was logosh, which was one reason Alexander had chosen Valentin for this duty. Valentin, in fact, was only half logosh. He could pass for human very well.

A commotion behind him made him turn. At the head of the receiving line, a young woman was crowing to Lady Hartwell at the top of her voice.

"What a *privilege* to be here, my lady. What an *honor*. Mrs. Cameron and I were so pleased by your *kind* invitation."

And there stood Mary, Valentin's Highland lady, just behind the girl, Mary's face set in tired patience. Valentin had no idea who the young woman was, nor who was the plump gentleman behind Mary, nor why Mary should be with them. He only saw her. *Here.*

A year fell away. Memories poured at him— Valentin lying in a stone chamber in a drafty Scottish castle, Mary leaning to tend him. Her bodice had been damp with the water she'd used to sponge his wound, her face beaded with perspiration. A tendril of dark hair had escaped her prim bun and stuck to her cheek, and he'd reached up to touch her.

She'd gasped, eyes widening. Then she'd, amazingly, leaned down to him and kissed him. Valentin had slid his hand behind her neck and held on while her breath swirled into his mouth and their lips had clung. He'd tasted her sweetness—Scottish honey and heady wine.

Later, he'd revealed all his secrets to her. Valentin had kissed her again, held her supple body against his. Now his heart beat in slow painful throbs as

Mary stood in stillness across the ballroom.

As her companions effused over Lord and Lady Hartwell, Mary turned to sweep the crowd with her gaze. Her eyes met Valentin's.

Everything stopped. Mary did not move, and neither did Valentin. Her hair was deep brown, candlelight catching its inner glow, and her dark blue bodice slid seductively from her shoulders. A man privileged to touch her could twine his arms around her waist, pull her against him, press his mouth to her bare throat.

Valentin's heartbeat thundered in his ears. After months of waiting and planning, torn by anger, impatience, and need, he at last stood in the same room with her.

Shrill female laughter cut through the polite chatter and strains of music from the orchestra. The young lady Mary had arrived with had moved to a knot of gentlemen, where she waved her fan and sashayed her hips.

Mary pressed her mouth closed and glided across the room, graceful as a doe, to fetch her. She took the young lady by the elbow and steered her out of the ballroom, the girl arguing every step of the way.

Valentin let out the breath he hadn't realized he'd been holding. Mary, here—*why?* Who were those people, and why did Mary behave as a mother would to the young lady?

Too much time had passed, so much had happened in Mary's life, and Valentin was no longer part of it. The thought burned through him like a slow match.

Someone bumped him. New lines of dancing had formed around Valentin, as he stood like a rock against the tide. The guests eyed him askance, wondering what the strange-looking foreigner was doing. Valentin took himself out of the way.

Then he cursed. Ambassador Rudolfo, the possible traitor whose every move Valentin was supposed to watch, was nowhere in sight.

Chapter Two

"THERE YOU ARE, MY BOY," Rudolfo called to Valentin in Nvengarian, as Valentin found his way into the upstairs card room.

The house was confusing, with many connected chambers, corridors, and courtyards, and it had taken Valentin a quarter of an hour to run Rudolfo to ground.

In this chamber, gentlemen and ladies clumped around tables, gazing at their cards in rapt concentration. Conversation was hushed, the focus on the game, the slap of cards punctuated with soft cries of victory or sighs of defeat. Above them on the walls, paintings of stiff gentlemen, women, and horses watched over all.

Duke Rudolfo clapped Valentin on the back, a habit Valentin already abhorred. "This is where our work is done in England, my lad. Over their games of whist and piquet and *vingt-un*. You lose gracefully at cards, and they eat from your hands. This is what Prince Damien tells me, in any case."

Rudolfo's mouth pulled into a slight sneer as he spoke Damien's name. Duke Rudolfo thought himself safe showing his disapproval of Nvengaria's Imperial Prince to Valentin—who had, once upon a time, been opposed to Damien himself.

Valentin, in fact, had gone so far as to attack Damien in his own palace, an event that had won him fame in the wrong quarters. This was another reason Grand Duke Alexander had given Valentin the assignment to watch Rudolfo—Rudolfo believed Valentin in sympathy with him, and therefore would be incautious.

Before Valentin could think of a reply, Duchess Wilhelmina swept into the card room. Behind her came Mary, the young woman in her charge, and the plump man Valentin had seen with them downstairs.

"Rudolfo," Duchess Wilhelmina sang out as she approached them. "This is Mary Cameron, sister of the most honorable Egan MacDonald of Scotland."

Rudolfo swiveled an admiring gaze to Mary's bosom and let it rest there as he took her offered hand and bowed over it. "Charmed, my lady."

Valentin fought his sudden logosh instinct to rip out Rudolfo's throat. Rudolfo liked to look at ladies, the more comely the better, and Mary was certainly comely.

Mary raised a sleek brow at him. "You are kind, Your Grace."

"No, do not be so formal," the ambassador boomed in painfully accented English. "Address me as Rudolfo, and my wife as Mina. You are friend to Nvengaria, no?"

Valentin half expected Mary to say, "No," very firmly. Through his anger, he wanted to laugh. Rudolfo would never take in Mary.

"My brother has said nothing but good things about Nvengaria," Mary replied smoothly. "And of course, Zarabeth, the prince's cousin, is now my sister-in-law."

No mention of Valentin. His temper flared. He would get an explanation out of her, make her tell him why she'd shunned him. Why she continued to shun him.

The young woman was bouncing on her toes. Mary introduced her to the ambassador and his wife as Miss Julia Lincolnbury and her father, Sir John. Rudolfo at least did not slide his lecherous gaze over Miss Lincolnbury. He had enough sense to leave virginal daughters alone, besides which, virgins bored him.

"Nvengarians, eh?" Sir John Lincolnbury said. "Funny, Nvengarians came up when I was looking over some of my investments in the City today. You buy much braid, you lot do. By the bucketful." He pointed at the gold trim adorning the ambassador's coat and glanced at Valentin, who wore his black military dress with plenty of braid on his shoulders. "You dress like soldiers, but there ain't no more war in Europe, now that we gave old Boney a kicking, eh?"

"Of course," Rudolfo said, unoffended. "The Nvengarian style of dress reminds us of old days, when we had to battle all the time to keep our country free of invaders. We still do this, if not so actively. That is why we have so many ambassadors."

He guffawed and Sir John chuckled with him, though it was clear Sir John did not truly understand what Rudolfo was talking about.

Duchess Mina suggested they sit down for cards.

The two gentlemen could play, she said, the so-charming Miss Lincolnbury could assist her, and Mary could stay with Baron Valentin and explain the games to him.

At last Mary came to life. "I am sorry, Your Grace, but Miss Lincolnbury has come to dance," she said, giving Duchess Mina a half bow. "We should return to the ballroom."

Miss Lincolnbury dug her fingers into Mary's arm and glared at her. Apparently playing cards with a duchess trumped dancing with young gentlemen—Valentin was not familiar enough with the ways of debutantes to know why.

Mary conceded reluctantly, and the duchess smiled and led Miss Lincolnbury away. Her husband followed with Rudolfo, leaving Mary alone with Valentin.

They faced each other for a long, frozen moment, Mary's color high, her breath rising in a long intake against the blue trim on her bodice.

Her eyes were dark brown, flecked with gold, framed with dark lashes. Entrancing, seductive. Mary never understood how deeply beautiful she was.

At the table about two feet from where Valentin and Mary stood, a man turned to blatantly stare at them. "You're breaking my concentration, old boy," he said to Valentin. "Have to keep my wits about me to prevent these ladies from beggaring me."

He spoke good-naturedly but also in a tone that said he expected Valentin, the foreigner and merely an ambassador's aide, to obey.

Valentin gave him a polite bow and led Mary to a small, empty table away from the others, where two chairs waited. He pulled out one chair and placed it in front of her. "Sit, please."

For a moment, he thought she'd refuse. She'd bathe him in scorn and sail out of the room, leaving Valentin holding a chair while these English people laughed at him.

But Mary was ever one for rigid politeness, whatever the circumstance. She sank gracefully into the chair, snapped open her fan, and flapped it vigorously.

Valentin seated himself across from her and reached for a card box in the middle of the table. It held three packs of cards, ready for any game.

"You will teach me." Valentin extracted a deck and laid it in front of Mary. "Perhaps the game of whist?"

Mary continued to wave her fan, avoiding looking at him directly. "You need four people for whist."

Valentin raised his brows as he stopped himself from restlessly ruffling the pack. "Is there is a game for two? In Nvengaria, we have *forzeqt*, for two, but it is very fast, very competitive. Sometimes bloody, when tempers are lost. Not, I think, a game for a London house." He heard himself babbling but for some reason couldn't make his tongue cease. Valentin, the man of few words, ran on in front of the woman he wanted to think highly of him.

Mary's expression didn't change. She was as poised as a statue, though much more vibrant. Everything about her was a song. "There is piquet," she said. "But for that we need a piquet deck."

"And this is not a piquet deck?"

Mary slammed her closed fan to the table and turned the pack over, her slender fingers separating the cards. "For piquet you use only seven through king, and aces."

Valentin could be silent on the matter most important to him no longer. His body was stiff as he leaned over the table and lowered his voice. "Why did you not come to me?"

Mary's hands stilled but she did not look up. "You have just betrayed how un-English you are." Her voice shook a little. "In this country, a gentleman would never dream of asking a lady an awkward question in so forthright a manner."

"But I am not English. And neither are you." Valentin balled his hands on the table. "Nvengarians do not cloak their feelings behind a mask of words."

Mary's gaze flicked to his at last. Her eyes were burning, emotions churning beneath her smooth surface. "No, you take out knives and go at each other in your Council meetings at the slightest provocation. Debating tax bills must be dreadfully exciting."

Valentin's hands tightened. "Such violence in government is a thing of the past now that Prince Damien rules."

"Then thank heavens for Prince Damien." Mary went back to extracting cards. "I am certain Nvengarian wives now feel much better about sending their husbands off to a day in government."

"Is that what you fear? The violent nature of Nvengarians?" Valentin tried to match her light tone. "I am not in any of the ruling councils, in any case."

Mary gathered the sorted cards into two piles and pushed one aside. "No, but Prince Damien sends you on missions where you get yourself shot."

Which he had while being bodyguard to Prince Damien's cousin at remote Castle MacDonald. "It was my duty to protect Princess Zarabeth."

Mary glanced across the room at Rudolfo and his

wife, now absorbed in a game with Miss Lincolnbury and her father. "At least this time your duty is no more dangerous than following an ambassador who has a roving eye."

Valentin said nothing. He slid the cards Mary had discarded to his side of the table and began to straighten them.

"Oh, dear," Mary said, her voice softening with sudden understanding. "It *is* dangerous, isn't it? That is why *you* were sent with him and not some mindless lackey."

Mary was an intelligent woman, one of the things Valentin loved about her. "I watch him," Valentin said, lifting his shoulders in a shrug. "It may come to nothing."

"But if it comes to something …?" Mary's intense gaze was on him again.

"Then I will do what I must."

"Which is?"

Valentin shook his head. "Too many ears."

"I understand." Mary heaved a sigh and began to shuffle what was left of the deck. A lock of hair fell from her coiffure and curved like a streak of midnight across her cheek. "Nvengarian secrets."

Valentin abandoned the cards he'd been toying with, reached across the table, and laid a heavy hand over hers. The words he had to say grated and hurt, but he had to push them out. "Why did you not come? Tell me."

A swallow moved down Mary's throat, but she did not jerk from him. "Back to forthright questions, are you?" She shook her head. "Please, do not ask me."

"I do ask you. I deserve to ask you."

Her fingers moved beneath his. "Nvengaria is

quite far away."

"Yes." Valentin held her gaze, his hand firming on hers.

"My son is here." Mary's voice became fainter. "At Cambridge."

"Yes." He continued to stare straight at her, willing her to tell him the truth.

Mary finally ceased toying with the pack. She set down the cards, her brown eyes troubled. "When we were in Scotland, you made me feel like a girl again." Her lashes flicked down, once, twice, as though she blinked back tears. "Full of hope, when for so long I'd known nothing but disappointment."

Valentin tried to understand. "And for this, you decided to stay home?"

She gave him an anguished look, and he saw that her eyes were indeed wet. "How could I go? Should I travel halfway across the continent to find that you'd forgotten me? That you meant nothing by your invitation? How could I risk that sort of humiliation?"

His heart beat faster in both frustration and hope. "Why did you not write me? I would have reassured you."

"Why did *you* not write?" Mary countered. "You ask a woman to travel a thousand miles to see you, but you cannot be bothered to mention whether you made it home safely yourself?"

"Princess Penelope and the Grand Duchess would have told you this," Valentin said, confused at her anger.

Mary looked heavenward and slid her hand from his. "I suppose I shouldn't be surprised that you behaved like a man."

"I am a man. Or half-man." Valentin paused. "Is

the fact that I am logosh what deterred you?"

She gave him a look of astonishment. "You believe I hesitated because you are *logosh*?"

Valentin shrugged. "You did not believe in logosh when I first came to Scotland. You believed in no magic at all. Nvengaria is a heavily magical place."

Mary laughed a little. "After the things that happened at my brother's castle I believe in magic, thank you very much."

Valentin's heart continued to beat rapidly, and his hands sweated inside his gloves. "Then may we begin again? I am whole and well now, and can be a fine lover to you."

Mary started, and her dark eyes widened. "Lover?"

Valentin warmed. "You are a beautiful woman, and I wish to offer you the pleasures of my bed."

"*Valentin.*" Mary leaned forward, the soft round of her bosom swelling against the table's edge. "You really must reread your book on English customs. A gentleman does not say such things to a lady in a room full of people. Not at all, in fact. Not if she's a lady."

Valentin's body began to tighten with pleasant heat. Mary was so near, after all this time, a touch away, and she was as passionate as ever. "The people in this room are playing cards and not listening. The ambassador commands their attention, not I."

Mary leaned closer. "Do not believe it. I have already overheard several bolder ladies speculating on what you look like out of your clothes."

Valentin smiled, thinking of how he'd stood with Mary outdoors on a cold Scottish night, without a stitch on him. "And did you tell them?"

Mary flushed and sat back. "No. Good heavens,

Valentin. What am I to do with you?"

Valentin stood. Before Mary could protest, he took her hand and tugged her up from her chair and with him to another door. Opening it, he slipped through, pulled her after him, closed the door, then turned before she could step away and pinned her against its panels.

"You will do *this* with me," he said, and kissed her.

Chapter Three

VALENTIN'S STRONG BODY HELD HER IN PLACE against the door while his hot tongue swept into her mouth. His hands found the curve of her waist, his grip strong, unrelenting.

He kissed her like he meant it, not as though he wanted to impress Mary with his tenderness or charm. He wanted her; she could taste it. No man had ever kissed her like Valentin.

Valentin eased his mouth from hers, but the panels of the door dug into her back, and his thighs were tight against hers. When Valentin had left Scotland a year ago, he'd been wan from his wound, but he'd grown healthy and sun-bronzed in the intervening months. Tonight he wore the formal midnight blue military uniform of Nvengaria, complete with gold braid, colorful medals, and slanting sash.

Mary couldn't help remembering the power of the body beneath the uniform, the muscles under his tight, warm skin. She'd seen all of Valentin's flesh, first when she'd nursed him, then again when she'd led him stealthily from the castle to the dark heath. He'd thrown off his clothes in order to shift into his wolf form, and for a moment, he'd stood bare, his body gleaming in the moonlight.

Valentin nuzzled the line of Mary's hair as he'd done that night in Scotland, as though he learned and memorized her scent.

"Do you propose to kiss me until I come with you to Nvengaria?" Mary whispered shakily.

Valentin smiled into her skin. "This does not seem so terrible a thing."

It did not seem terrible to Mary, either. "If it were as simple as kisses, I would have left Scotland long ago. But it is not that easy."

Valentin's blue eyes flickered as he drew back. He'd shaved recently, his hard jaw smooth rather than sanded with whiskers as she remembered it. He'd grown strong again, like the rock cliffs on which Castle MacDonald was built.

"It *is* simple," he said. "But perhaps I want too much."

Valentin's voice had always been mesmerizing. Mary had forgotten in the intervening months how full and deep was his timbre, how rich his accent, how he pronounced each English word as though he did not want to make a mistake.

She'd been praising herself for allowing Julia and her father to persuade her to come with them to the ball despite the fact that Valentin would be here, but now she wondered if she shouldn't have ignored Julia's pleas and stayed home. She'd thought she could stand resolute but she was already crumpling.

"I barely know you," Mary said, the tremor in her voice lingering. "I'd only just learned who and what you were, and then you were gone." Taking Mary's peace of mind — what little she'd had — with him.

Valentin closed his hands over her shoulders. She loved the hard heat of his body against hers, his breath on her lips. "Then you will learn more of me, as I stay to watch my ambassador."

Uneasiness trickled through her. "Is Duke Rudolfo so dangerous?" He'd seemed rather harmless, if a bit crude. "Is that why you're watching him?"

"The Grand Duke is suspicious of him." Valentin spoke with conviction. "That is enough for me."

Mary nodded. "Yes, I remember Grand Duke Alexander. A formidable man. Icy and precise." Tall and eagle-eyed, Grand Duke Alexander was reputed to be the iron hand inside charming Prince Damien's velvet glove. So Mary had heard, and she believed it.

"The Grand Duke is the most dangerous man in Europe," Valentin went on. "So if *he* worries that a man wishes to destroy Nvengaria, I too worry."

Mary touched Valentin's face, seeking the lines she'd tried so hard to forget. She was suddenly angry on his behalf. "It is not fair that they always send *you* to face their troubles."

Valentin gave his characteristic shrug. "I am good at it."

Mary's blood heated. "If I asked you to tell them, no, you will not endanger yourself for them — would you?"

He didn't hesitate long. "No." Something glinted in his eyes, determination, regret, before it was gone.

There it was, then. Valentin would not unbend for her, nor she for him. And Mary was no longer the bending sort.

Valentin brushed a tendril of hair from her face, his touch so warm her knees began to buckle. "The ambassador's wife wishes to be friends with you. It would help me if you let her."

Mary blinked. "Help you?"

"In my task."

Mary smiled to mask her hurt. "Ah, you mean will I cultivate her friendship and give you the juicy gossip she spills about her husband?"

"I would not ask were it not important," Valentin said. "The safety of Nvengaria, and perhaps England as well, might depend on it."

"That important, is it?" Mary made a gesture of resignation. "You know that as a Scotswoman I would cheerfully watch England sink into the sea, as long as the Stone of Destiny washed up again on our shores." She sighed. "But then I have many English friends I would not like to see hurt. Nvengarians as well. I will help you for their sake."

"Thank you." Valentin sounded relieved.

Mary kissed him lightly on the chin, pretending his warm skin under her lips didn't make her heart pound. "You could have convinced me to help you without the kiss. Not that it wasn't pleasant."

Valentin frowned as he continued to trace her cheek, his left hand remaining on her waist. "My feelings for you have nothing to do with the ambassador. I would stay here with you all night, showing you what I want with you, but I should not leave him for long."

Mary's already quick heartbeat sped again, heat suffusing her limbs. *I would stay here all night, showing you what I want with you.* A dangerous thing to tell her—her imagination was too creative. "Now I know why the Grand Duke sent you," she said, her tone light. "You are good at flattering others to help you."

Valentin's frown deepened. "I would never flatter

to gain help. That smacks of deceit, and I tired of that long ago."

Mary wondered what he meant by this and realized anew that she knew so little about Valentin. He was younger than she, but she wasn't certain how much younger. She knew nothing at all of his life in Nvengaria, and her Nvengarian friends had surprisingly little information about him.

She softened her voice and let her hand drift to the medals pinned to his broad chest. "Of course I will help. I understand the seriousness of your task. I will befriend Mina, as she wants me to call her, and report all she tells me. As the ambassador says, I am a good friend to Nvengaria. Perhaps we should return to the duke and his wife now, before they plot any assassinations."

"It is not a laughing matter. The ambassador might do just that."

Mary felt a qualm. "Forgive me. You are right. Nvengarian politics, from what I have seen, are exciting but deadly. I've promised to help. We should go now."

Instead of releasing her, Valentin cupped her face with his hand, his thumb warm on her cheeks. His eyes held concern, wariness, and a vast watchfulness that she'd noticed in him before. He could be as volatile as any of his countrymen—she'd seen that in him when he'd hunted for kidnappers last year. But he was also very good at containing his violence, honing it until it became as quiet and deadly as a sword.

Valentin kissed her lips, his touch almost gentle. "Thank you," he said, and finally let her go.

* * *

THE NEXT DAY MARY, JULIA, AND SIR JOHN rolled

from the Lincolnbury house in Curzon Street to a Grosvenor Square mansion by invitation of the Nvengarian ambassador and his wife. Julia was excited, reasoning that acquaintanceship with a duchess, even a foreign duchess, would carry much weight when she entered her second Season in the spring. Julia had fussed over what to wear until Mary had nearly gone mad, but as they traveled the short distance to the ambassador's residence, Mary found herself becoming as nervous as Julia.

Mary had fretted over her own appearance, but for a different reason. She'd peered anxiously into her mirror for a good half hour before she'd finally gone to round up Julia, wondering if the fine lines at the corners of her eyes were entirely noticeable. Perhaps she should cover them with powder.

She'd made herself turn from the mirror in self-disapproval. Was she that vain?

She was, if a little powder meant Valentin would not notice how elderly she was becoming. But he would discover the lines sooner or later, especially if he kissed her as he had in the anteroom. He likely had already noticed them.

In the end, Mary left off the powder, but dared to touch her cheeks with the tiniest hint of rouge.

As Mary suspected, this was not to be an intimate visit with Duke Rudolfo and his wife. When they entered the ambassador's mansion, two other English gentlemen Mary did not know, along with their wives, already strolled about the drawing room. Julia looked dismayed until she realized she was the only young and unmarried lady present.

The gentlemen retired to the billiards room, leaving the ladies to tea and the pianoforte in the high-ceilinged drawing room. Long windows brought in winter light to touch gold highlights to the French chairs, delicate tea tables, and ladies' gowns. Mary sat at the satinwood Sheraton pianoforte at Duchess Mina's insistence, having heard that Mary played well.

Mary let her fingers take her through a Mozart minuet while her gaze strayed to the partly open door to the adjoining billiards room. The click of balls and sound of male voices drifted from it, but Mary was aware only of Valentin, who'd discarded his coat to play in shirtsleeves. The half-open door gave Mary tantalizing and maddening glimpses of him leaning over the table to shoot.

Mary forced herself to pay attention to the keyboard for a difficult passage, pleased at the way the notes tripped from her fingertips. Mary had excelled at music as a girl and had mourned when her husband's gambling debts had taken away her beloved pianoforte. She'd practiced some at the Lincolnburys' these past weeks, but this instrument—finely built and well tuned—was a joy to play.

When Mary lifted her head again, Valentin was standing in the doorway of the billiards room, his cue upright beside him. Without his coat, his shirt clung to his torso, his Nvengarian uniform having no waistcoat. Mary fumbled a chord, her heart thrumming.

Valentin watched until she reached the end of the piece. The ladies clapped, Julia with enthusiasm. Valentin said nothing at all. He gave Mary a long look then turned silently and went back to the game.

Julia came to the pianoforte, still clapping, and slid to the bench beside Mary. "Tell me what I should play, Aunt Mary. Something the duchess will like."

She meant something she would not mangle too embarrassingly. Mary sorted through the music on top of the instrument until she found an easy piece Julia already knew. She laid it out for her then rose and left Julia to it.

Duchess Mina smiled at Mary and patted the cushions on the sofa next to her. Julia launched into her piece rather loudly, and Mary sat down, her hands hurting for some reason. She must have held them too stiffly on the keys.

Duchess Mina leaned to her and spoke into her ear. "I saw him watching you. Valentin, I mean. It is difficult for him."

Mary glanced at the other ladies of the party, but they sat together on another sofa, their full and polite attention on Julia. "Difficult?" Mary whispered in return.

"That piece you played. It was a favorite of his sister's."

"Valentin has a sister?" Mary asked in amazement. She'd never heard anything about a sister.

"No more, my dear," Duchess Mina said, sounding mournful. "Her name was Sophie. She died, poor thing, when Valentin was about twenty."

"Oh." Mary stilled in disquiet. "I didn't know. How sad."

"It was more than sad. It was terrible." The duchess lowered her voice still more. "Our old Imperial Prince came to call one day when Valentin was not at home. Valentin had been sent away by the Imperial Prince himself, on 'official' business, so the prince said. The prince found Sophie alone and expected her to show him *hospitality*." Duchess Mina leaned closer. "If you know what I mean."

Mary hesitated, worry rippling through her. "I am not certain I do."

"Ah, my dear, you English are so innocent."

"I am Scottish," Mary murmured.

"I mean he wished to seduce her." Mina gave her a knowing look. "Valentin's sister resisted, as you might expect, so the old prince, he took what he wanted. No one refused the Imperial Prince anything." Duchess Mina shook her head. "He let his manservant have her afterward, to punish her for being so stubborn. Sophie could not live with the shame. Not many days later, she took her own life. I do not blame her for this."

Mary put her hand to her throat in shock. "Dear heavens. Poor Valentin. He never told me."

"He does not speak about it, no. But his need for vengeance runs deep." Duchess Mina put her open fan between them and the rest of the room. "Valentin's hatred for the Imperial family of Nvengaria is great also. It is said he will stop at nothing to destroy every last one of them."

This was news to Mary. "I know he once tried to assassinate Prince Damien. But he has reconciled with Damien, hasn't he? He escorted Damien's cousin to Scotland last year, where she married my brother. Zarabeth has only high praise for Valentin."

"He bides his time, my dear." Duchess Mina looked wise. "My husband, Rudolfo, he so worries about Valentin. Of all the men the Grand Duke could have sent with us to England, he chose Valentin. To remove Valentin from Nvengaria perhaps? Was he plotting something against Damien again?"

Mary thought carefully before she replied. She had learned enough about Nvengarian politics from Zarabeth to know they were never straightforward.

Nvengarians could have a dozen different loyalties and choose which one best suited the moment without thinking themselves inconsistent. Gossip and whispers were effective campaigns in destroying a rival. Valentin had warned Mary to watch the ambassador—now the ambassador's wife was telling her to watch Valentin.

"Valentin must miss his sister very much," Mary ventured.

"Of course he does, dear. He keeps much to himself."

Julia's piece came to an end. Duchess Mina dropped her fan and applauded, and Mary followed suit.

"Most excellent," Duchess Mina crooned to Julia. "Your playing, it is delightful. Now, you must sit next to me and tell me all about your English Christmas customs. Your king has given us the use of a house in Hertfordshire, and I intend to celebrate a very English Christmas this year. I want to know everything about the Yule log and the bowl of wassail and maids stealing the footmen's trousers."

Julia went off into a peal of laughter, and Mary raised her brows.

"But is this not so?" the duchess asked, not the least bit embarrassed. "I read that if the footman does not fill the house with holly on the day of Christmas, the maids may take his trousers."

Mary fought the urge to laugh as loudly as Julia. "I am afraid we never practiced such a thing at Castle MacDonald."

"But Aunt Mary is Scottish," Julia said, as though this made Mary backward and untutored. "Men there don't wear trousers. They wear skirts."

"Kilts," Mary corrected her.

The duchess smiled a sly smile. "Yes, I have seen these Scottish men. Your brother, Mrs. Cameron, he wears the kilt, no? And Baron Valentin has told us about your customs—the black bun, and the first-footed man, and other intriguing things."

"Not all of which is practiced in England," Mary said quickly.

"No matter." The duchess smiled all around, her ingenuousness vivid. "Miss Lincolnbury, you must come to my house in Hertfordshire and show me how to be very English. We will have some Scottish things too, and on Twelfth Night have the—how do you call him?—the Lord of Un-rule?"

"*Mis*rule," Julia said. "You put a bean in a cake, and whoever gets it in his piece is the lord for the night. Everyone must obey him no matter what madness he suggests."

"Excellent." The duchess clapped her hands. "We have a similar custom in Nvengaria, but our Lord of Misrule commands that all ladies must kiss him."

Julia giggled. "Oh, I think I should like Nvengarian customs."

"Then it is settled." Mina beamed at them. "You will come. I go tomorrow to be ready for Christmas Day."

Julia's face fell. "But I cannot. Papa has many meetings in the City, to do with his importing business, I think. We are staying in London for Christmas."

Duchess Mina looked undaunted. "That is easy enough. Mrs. Cameron can accompany you, can she not? My husband, he stays in London as well, to do business with your king, but he will join us when he is able. He will speak to your father. I'm sure all will be well."

Mary glanced at the billiards room. Framed by the open doorway, Valentin bent over the table, his body like a taut spring. He lined up his cue with the precision of a hunter, then made a sudden, tight shot. Balls clacked and rolled into pockets, and the other men groaned and backed from the table.

Mary's heart sped as Valentin turned away, lost to her sight. If the ambassador remained in London, so would Valentin. That meant Mary would see little of him for the remainder of her visit to England. At New Year's she would return to Scotland, leaving London and Valentin behind.

Which was what she wanted. Wasn't it?

She waffled. "I expect my son from Cambridge any day now. He will look for me in London."

Duchess Mina waved that aside. "Send him a letter and invite him to Hertfordshire. He can attend us ladies."

Julia gave Mary an imploring look. "*Please,* Aunt Mary? Hertfordshire is ever so much closer to Cambridge than London anyway. Just think how it will be if I can tell everyone I spent Christmas with a *duchess.*"

It would be a social feather in plain Miss Lincolnbury's cap, true. The visit would also enable Mary to watch the duchess and learn what she could about the ambassador, as she had told Valentin she would. She smothered a sigh.

"Very well, Julia. I will ask your father."

Julia flung herself to her knees and hugged Mary's lap. "Thank you. *Thank* you. You are the best aunt in the entire world. Even if you aren't really my aunt."

Mary looked up to see Valentin at the doorway again, his blue eyes quiet but his body tense. He nodded once at her, as though she'd made the correct choice, and turned away

* * *

WHEN MARY DEPARTED LATER WITH JULIA and Sir John, Valentin, coat restored, saw them into the coach. He said nothing to Mary, but she felt the rough edges of a folded paper press against her gloved palm as he handed her in. He stepped back to let a footman slam the door, while Duchess Mina waved them off like an excited schoolgirl.

Mary kept the note hidden until they reached the Lincolnbury house in Curzon Street, treasuring it as though it were a diamond Valentin had bought especially for her.

When she opened the message in the privacy of her bedchamber she found one cryptic line in a slanted but precise handwriting. *Meet me,* it read and told her exactly where and when.

Mary held the paper to her lips, her heart burning.

Chapter Four

VALENTIN'S BREATH QUICKENED WHEN he saw Mary striding toward him through the lowering fog in Hyde Park. The sun was setting and the weather was cold, but she walked steadily in her sensible cloak and hood. Practical Mary. The cloak would hide her identity from the casual passer-by as well as warm her.

A prim looking woman followed a discreet distance behind her. Mary's maid, he guessed. A respectable widow could not be seen walking about alone, especially near dark.

"Can she be trusted?" Valentin asked, glancing at the maid as Mary stopped beside him.

"A good evening to you too," Mary answered in her crisp voice. She took his offered arm and strolled with him down a path that led across a wide green. The park spread out to their left, offering a view of horses and carriages on the Rotten Row.

Valentin liked the feel of Mary's gloved hand on

his arm, her body warming his side. Her plaid skirt rippled from beneath her cloak as she walked. MacDonald plaid, the symbol of her clan.

"Yes, I trust her," Mary said once they'd left the maid behind. "She's Scots and loyal to my family. She might disapprove of my behavior and tell me so bluntly, but she would never spread tales outside the family. I read your note. What is this clandestine meeting all about?"

"Where is Hertfordshire?" Valentin asked abruptly.

Mary's brows arched. "You bade me meet you in secret to ask where Hertfordshire is? Would it not have been simpler to consult a map?"

Valentin let her teasing flow past him, enjoying the sound of her voice no matter what she said. "The duchess mentioned her plans for her English Christmas, but I have not seen this house she speaks of. Is Hertfordshire far from London?"

"No, it is only a few hours north, and quite picturesque as I recall." Mary smiled faintly, the corners of her mouth pulling. "The duchess longs to skate on a pond and savor English country Christmas traditions."

"You will go with her?"

"Julia wants to." Mary shrugged. "I admit, it would be good for her. Julia is not wrong that making friends with an ambassador's wife will raise her worth on the marriage mart."

Valentin watched horses and riders on the Row fade into the fog. "You speak of marriage so coldly."

Mary was silent for a time, as though thinking this through. "I made the mistake of marrying for love— passion, rather," she said, her voice quiet. "I hope Julia never does the same."

"It is not your fault that your husband turned out to be a fool," Valentin said, barely containing his temper. He'd heard about Mary's husband from her brother and her nephew, Jamie.

Mary looked up at him, her eyes tight. "You are blunt."

Valentin's anger burned like a low flame, a rage that twisted him and stirred old pain. "He hurt you and left you destitute. You had to beg for help from your brother."

Mary lifted her chin. "Egan was happy to have me live again at Castle MacDonald. And I never begged."

Valentin softened his voice. "No. Not you." He imagined Mary standing ramrod straight in front of her brother as she explained that her husband had died penniless and that Egan was stuck with her. It must have shattered her spirit to do even that.

"In Nvengaria it is considered honorable to marry for passion," Valentin said as they walked along. "We prize love over riches. If a marriage must be arranged for political reasons, it is agreed that both parties can fulfill their desires with whomever they wish outside the marriage, without retribution."

Mary's look turned wry. "Gracious, how very convenient."

Even her pointed observation sounded musical. "I would not know," Valentin said, resting his hand over hers where it lay on his arm. "I never married."

"Why not?" Mary sounded curious. "Did you never find someone who ignited your passion?"

"Not until I went to Scotland." The words came out of him—truth.

Mary flushed and looked away. "You tease me. I am a widow of five-and-thirty and have a son who has started at Cambridge."

They took a turning to a damp, narrow walk screened by hedges, where light fog wove ghostly fingers through bare branches.

Valentin sensed that Mary expected an answer, but he was not certain what to say. He'd never been eloquent. "These things, they are part of who you are," was all he could manage when the silence had stretched too long.

"How old are *you*, Valentin? I never asked."

Valentin had to calculate; he so little thought about such things. "Seven-and-twenty as the English would say it. But I am logosh."

Mary raised her brows in surprise. "What has that to do with anything?"

"Full logosh are considered men at fifteen, ready to take a mate and produce offspring. In Britain your son does not even begin university until he is seventeen and he does not reach his—how do you say it?—majority—until he is one-and-twenty."

"And then he goes on his Grand Tour." Mary's smile was strained. "Before he even considers taking a wife. My husband was seven-and-twenty when he married me, the same age you are now. Only I was seventeen, making my first bow. And now here I am, a widow walking alone with a young, dashing, ambassador's aide. What a scandal."

Valentin leaned to study her face under the hood, taking in her scent trapped by her cloak. "Nvengarians would not consider us a scandal at all. They would celebrate it."

Mary swallowed. "Well, I am not Nvengarian. And I have a son to consider."

Valentin halted, pulling her to face him. They stood alone on the path, the cold wind blocked by the tall hedges, the maid, discreet indeed, nowhere in sight. "Do you think I would shame you by creating scandal for you?" he asked, anger stirring. "That I value you so little?"

By the pain in her eyes, Mary did think that. "Duchess Mina told me what happened to your sister."

The words were not ones Valentin expected to hear, and he wondered why Mary spoke of Sophie now, without preamble.

His body tightened. "Why did the duchess tell you this?"

"I'm not certain, really," she answered, sounding puzzled. "I suppose she wanted to explain that you lived to take your revenge and nothing more."

An image of Sophie rose in Valentin's mind, the one he always saw. His sister's blue eyes sparkled with laughter, with her vibrant love of life. Sophie had remained lighthearted even as they'd watched their fortune dwindle and the house grow colder and shabbier each year. It didn't matter, she'd said. They still had each other.

Remembering Sophie hurt like the devil, but Valentin never tried to push thoughts of her away.

"She was lovely," he said, his voice gentling. "You would have liked her."

"If she was anything like you, yes, I think I would have." Mary put a warm hand on his arm. "I am so sorry, Valentin."

Valentin swallowed the ache in his throat. "The ambassador's wife is correct only in part. I tried to kill Prince Damien in vengeance for my sister. As I was not given the opportunity to kill his father, I thought to destroy his son. In Nvengaria, we are willing to take one family member in payment for another."

He felt Mary's shiver. "But Damien talked you out of it."

Valentin nodded, remembering the day he'd crept into the palace, knife hard under his coat, ready to both kill and die. He'd managed to get all the way into the Imperial Prince's private rooms, to take the place of one of the servers at his dinner table, to stand behind Damien's chair. He'd lifted his dagger to drive it into Damien's neck.

Damien's wife Penelope, a young Englishwoman, had seen and screamed, and Damien had dived aside just in time. Valentin's blade had slashed Damien's coat, missing the prince by a hair's breadth. And then Damien's bodyguards had piled on Valentin and dragged him away.

Valentin had been thrown into a cell. They'd known somehow that he was half logosh, and had reinforced the cell against his unnatural strength. They'd let him stew a few days, and then Prince Damien himself had come to talk to him. Every day.

Valentin had been sullen at first, refusing to speak, but gradually he'd opened up. Valentin found himself telling Damien about Sophie, what the now-dead Imperial Prince had done to his family, and about all his rage and grief.

Eventually Valentin had come to understand that Damien was intelligent, shrewd, generous-hearted, and wise, very different from his horrible father. Valentin had grown to respect and then to like Damien.

"Prince Damien can talk very well," Valentin said with a touch of amusement. "He is, as you say, a raconteur. But it was his wife's love for him that convinced me I had it wrong. She is pure of heart and could not love a monster."

Mary gave him an assessing look. "Then your quest for vengeance is over? And the duchess is mistaken?"

Valentin nodded. "My quest is of a different kind now."

Her gaze remained shrewd. "To catch the ambassador doing something that will condemn him?"

Valentin slid his arms around Mary's waist. "My quest was to find a woman with eyes the color of chocolate." The soft round of her breasts pressed his coat, and Valentin lowered his head to lick the hollow of her throat. Her skin was salty, warm from their walk.

"Valentin." Mary's voice was a whisper.

"I do not ask lightly." Valentin raised his head and pushed her hood back, letting his lips skim the line of her hair. "I want you as my lover. To give you all that the word means."

He felt her shiver again. "While you are in London, fulfilling your task of spying on the ambassador?"

"For as long as you'll have me."

Valentin sensed the strain in her, the fear, saw it in her eyes. "Now, we're speaking again of me traveling to Nvengaria, a land I know nothing of. I've never been farther from home than Brighton, and I didn't think much of that."

Valentin touched her hair, loving the silk of it. "Do you wait for me to offer marriage?"

Mary shook her head. She broke his hold and walked on, her plaid skirts brushing his legs as she passed him.

Valentin caught up to her with ease. "The reason I

do not offer marriage is because I have nothing," he said, truth tumbling out again. "My estate is bankrupt. I lost everything even before my sister died. It was one reason the Imperial Prince could not understand why Sophie resisted him. He offered to clear our debts—which he had caused in the first place. My father had made him his enemy."

Anger flared on Mary's face, and Valentin liked that anger. She understood. "The loathsome man," she said in a ringing voice. "I do hope he died painfully."

"Rumors say that Grand Duke Alexander poisoned him, but no one has proved it." Valentin shook his head. "No one wishes to." There were many rumors about the old prince's death, but no investigation had come from it. Everyone was simply relieved the evil old man had gone.

"I can believe it of the ruthlessly efficient Grand Duke Alexander," Mary said decidedly. "But surely Alexander can help restore your estate. As can Prince Damien, if he has become so pleased with you."

"The Grand Duke pays for my services, but not enough to keep a wife." Valentin took Mary's hand and turned her to him again. "I know that your husband left you destitute. I would never saddle you with another penniless husband."

A fleeting smile touched her face. "Mr. Cameron was not so much penniless as profligate. You seem the frugal sort."

"Mary." Valentin lifted her hand to his lips. "I can offer you so little."

"That's not true, you know." Her dark eyes sparkled in the winter light. "You can offer yourself."

But for Valentin, that was not enough. He wanted to give her everything a beautiful woman should have: gowns, jewels, horses, a grand carriage, a beautiful house full of beautiful things. He wanted her to be the envy of every lady in Nvengaria—*he* wanted to be the envy of every gentleman that he had such a lady on his arm.

"I do offer myself." Valentin pressed firm kisses on each of her fingers, then held her hand against his own cheek. "My friends would think you prudent for not tying yourself to me in marriage. You would be free to leave at any time, free to live your own life, with your own money."

Mary blinked. "Let me understand you. You are saying that people in Nvengaria live together openly, without marriage, and consider it *prudent*?"

He nodded. "If a woman risked beggaring herself by marrying, yes."

She let out a breath. "This Nvengaria is a strange place."

"It is a beautiful place." Mary would love it— knife-sharp mountains, deep blue lakes, emerald meadows that were a carpet of brilliant flowers in the spring. "Nvengarians would also think you prudent because I am logosh. They are still not comfortable with wild creatures in their midst."

Mary looked away. "Neither am I, to tell you the truth." Her voice was soft, uncertain.

Valentin ran his thumb across the backs of her fingers in her skintight leather gloves. "Then it would be wise for you not to marry me."

Mary disengaged her hand and shook her head. "You've run mad, you know. You wish me to travel with you to Nvengaria—whenever your duty here ends—and live with you openly as your mistress. So that the allowance my brother gives me will keep me well in your drafty house, and if your ability to change into a wolf becomes too much for me, I can leave with impunity."

Valentin nodded. "Yes. To all of that."

She gave him a narrow look. "You do realize that most Englishwomen would consider your offer not only shocking but a grave insult? They'd be swooning in the space of a moment."

"Would they?" The English never ceased to amaze him.

Mary's mouth curved, and her eyes filled with wicked beauty. "How fortunate for you that I am Scottish."

Hope flared in his heart. "Then you will agree?"

"I mean I will give it careful consideration." Mary turned from him again. This time Valentin let her walk away, liking how her cloak flowed over the curve of her hips.

After a few yards, Mary turned back. "I refuse to believe that you arranged this assignation simply to make your shocking proposal," she said, cocking her head. "Why did you truly wish to meet?"

Chapter Five

VALENTIN NO LONGER WANTED TO TALK about business. He felt light, almost giddy, with the possibility that Mary would throw everything to the wind and return with him to Nvengaria. He'd show her his world, see that she loved it as he did. They could travel to Scotland from there anytime she wanted — there was beauty in that land too.

He forced himself back to the matter at hand and moved to stand near Mary again. He did not reach for her, but he let his leg touch the fold of her skirt. "I wish to ask you about Miss Lincolnbury's father," he said.

Mary's brows rose sharply. "Sir John? What about him?"

"Who is he? What sort of business does he conduct, and why is he here in London over Christmas?"

"Goodness, is that all?" Mary gave him a shrewd look. "Why do you wish to know?"

"Because Ambassador Rudolfo seems interested in him. More than a Nvengarian duke should be interested in a plain English baronet."

Valentin did not understand why Rudolfo seemed determined to find out all about Sir John, and this gnawed at him. As they'd played billiards, Rudolfo had questioned Sir John about everything — why he'd come to London for the winter, what house he'd hired, where his estate was in the north of England, what he did in the country. Valentin had looked on, watchful.

That is, until he'd been drawn to watching Mary play. The tune she'd chosen had been Sophie's favorite, which Valentin had not been able to listen to since her death. He'd been known to rise and leave concert rooms when it was played, unable to bear it.

Under Mary's fingers, the piece had taken a different nature. It had become beautiful again, a fond memory rather than a thing to tear at him.

Mary was giving him a thoughtful look. "Duchess Mina too seems quite interested in Julia. I am fond of Julia and Sir John for my friend Allison's sake, but they are not among the great and titled. Though Sir John is very rich."

"How did he make this money? Is he in employ of your government?"

Mary shook her head. "Allison — Sir John's late wife — told me his wealth came from family money and good investments," she said. "He is forever going to the City and the Corn Exchange, and Julia will become a very wealthy young lady upon her majority. I'm certain the gentlemen will come out of the woodwork for Julia then," she finished cynically.

"I wondered if Rudolfo wishes Sir John to be his liaison to the English government," Valentin said. "A way for the ambassador to betray Nvengarian secrets."

Mary looked skeptical. "If so, Ambassador Rudolfo could choose a better conspirator. Sir John is a kind man, and Allison loved him, but he's not very bright, except when it comes to money. He has a knack there."

"Hmm. Perhaps he is the exact kind of man the ambassador needs. One known to be slow-witted and innocent. Who would suspect him?"

Mary's eyes widened. "Goodness, you see plots everywhere. Perhaps the ambassador and his wife simply like Sir John and Julia. The duke and duchess seem a bit slow-witted themselves."

"When Nvengaria is involved there *are* plots everywhere," Valentin said darkly. "And conspirators and spies."

"Like you." Mary smiled.

Her smile could stop his heart. It made him want to be the best man in the world—honorable, noble, virtuous, and wealthy for her sake. Valentin was none of those things.

If he could hold Mary in his arms, bury himself in her, breathe her scent all night, he was certain he would be well again. His wounds might heal, and Valentin might forget, for just a little while, how he'd failed everyone in his life.

"Like me," he agreed in a quiet voice.

He'd kissed her at the ball last night in a fever of longing. His longing was no less today, but he wanted to take things slowly this time. Valentin leaned down, and Mary readily lifted herself to him, their mouths meeting in for long, hot kiss.

I need you to make me whole, he wanted to say. Did he have the right to ask that of her?

Mary slid her arms around Valentin's neck. Her lips were warm in the cold December air, the heat in her mouth as he kissed her a haven. He loved the sharp taste of her, like cinnamon and exotic spices.

He eased the kiss to its end. "Be with me, Mary," he said. "*Please.*"

The sudden longing in her eyes wasn't masked. But then Mary looked stricken and shook her head. "I can't. Not right now. I am Julia's chaperone. If I do anything untoward, I could compromise her chances."

Valentin's temper splintered. "In Scotland, you were tied to no one. You were ready to leave the castle to your brother and Zarabeth. Now I find you with these people you do not even respect. When will you free yourself to simply be *Mary*?"

Mary flushed. "Julia is the daughter of my closest friend, who died some years ago. Julia needs help, and I will not let her drift. I owe it to Allison."

"You like to tie yourself to needy people," Valentin said, unable to stop the blunt words. "They take advantage of you."

"That might be true." Mary's voice softened. "But it's nice to be needed."

"*I* need you," he growled.

Mary clasped Valentin's arms, her fingers closing firmly on him. "You are the strongest man I know." Her dark eyes held conviction, hope, clarity, and a watchfulness. "You take care of everyone—Zarabeth, the ambassador, Prince Damien. When will you release yourself to be *Valentin*?"

Valentin's throat tightened. "It is not the same thing. I am atoning for my past."

"For trying to stab Prince Damien? I thought you'd been forgiven that."

"Not for Damien," Valentin said impatiently. "For Sophie."

"How on earth are you to blame for that?" Mary's tone held incredulity. "From what I understand, no one could stop the old Imperial Prince from doing whatever he wanted."

Valentin shook his head, his eyes stinging. "I was not there to defend her. I'd gone off and left Sophie alone."

"Not alone, surely," practical-minded Mary said. "I imaging you had servants and bodyguards in your house. Every Nvengarian nobleman and noblewoman has bodyguards, I've been given to understand."

"If they'd tried to stand against the Imperial Prince, he'd have had them shot." Valentin's heart burned with fierce fire. "Sophie knew that. She wouldn't let them stop him."

Tears trickled down his face, hot on his cold skin. Englishmen avoided showing emotion, but Nvengarians were not ashamed to weep.

He saw Mary's anguished face before her arms were around him. Her embrace held heat against the winter day, the fur of her cloak tickling his cheek. Her body against his comforted him as though he floated without care in a warm sea.

The feeling of her heart beating between her breasts soothed his hurt a little. Valentin pressed his lips to her neck and absorbed the warmth trapped inside her cloak.

If he could stay in Mary's arms forever, all would be well. He was certain of it.

* * *

MARY'S MIND SPUN WITH CONFLICTING thoughts the rest of the evening and through the long winter night, and on into morning as she finished packing Julia's things for the visit to Hertfordshire.

The pain in Valentin's eyes when he'd spoken of his sister had been raw. Mary ached for him, had felt the heartbreak in him when she'd held him. She'd wanted to keep on holding him as the park darkened, wanting to soothe him until he ceased shaking.

But he'd raised his head, wiping his eyes of his unashamed tears, and conceded that they needed to return home before either of them was gone too long.

Valentin had walked her to the edge of the park, her disapproving maid trailing them, his body tall and strong next to hers, and handed her into a hackney coach to take her back to Sir John's Curzon Street house. He'd touched her fingers as he'd withdrawn to let her ride in the hackney without him, the look in his eyes as tender as his kisses.

A man who knew how to love. Who wanted her as his lover.

Those two thoughts kept Mary awake most of the night and had her sandy-eyed and impatient the next morning.

Mary and Julia rode to Hertfordshire with Duchess Mina in a traveling coach that was a decadence of cushions and velvet upholstery. Ingenious fold-down cabinets contained food, drink, books, and magazines, everything the well-heeled traveler could want. Punched tin boxes of glowing coals warmed their feet. The duchess even had a hand-warmer—a small metal box wrapped in a cloth with a bit of coal inside—tucked into her muff. She generously let Julia use the warmer when Julia complained of cold fingers.

The morning was cold and crisp, the sky bright

blue, the air dry and clear. Perfect for a journey out of the city. Pristine English countryside unfolded around them as the four horses in gleaming harness jogged along. Hedge-lined lanes led through a patchwork quilt of small farms; woods and gentle hills flowed to the horizon.

Julia and the duchess exclaimed at the prettiness. Mary, used to rugged Scottish mountains that dropped into churning seas, found the scenery tame and a bit dull.

The house in Hertfordshire was breathtaking. Good King George must have wished to keep the Nvengarians happy, because he'd given them an enormous Palladian mansion that rose, escarpment-like, from a vast snow-covered lawn. The extensive park ran to woods to the east, and a frozen pond glimmered like a fallen mirror across the grounds to the west before it bent out of sight around a stand of trees.

The park even had a ha-ha—a green bank, now dusted with snow, that rose gently to end in an abrupt drop. A trespasser dashing across the great English lord's land in the middle of the night would suddenly find himself falling five feet down, landing flat on his face in the mud. *Ha, ha.*

Mary disapproved. Scottish castles were open to the entire clan, places to gather in times of trouble and equally for celebration. English houses, beautiful to look at, shut out all but the privileged few.

The house inside was a typical stately home, with high-ceilinged rooms, a central elegant staircase, myriad halls, and paintings of two hundred years of the house's inhabitants. As they entered, the butler informed the duchess that the pond was indeed safe for skating. The duchess squealed and clapped her hands in excitement.

It was the twenty-first of December, Yule, the longest night. They would have a skating party this afternoon, Duchess Mina declared, and then they'd burn the Yule log and have all kinds of festivities after dark. The ambassador had said he could join them that evening, and he'd bring Julia's father with him. It would be a fine celebration.

That meant Valentin would come. Mary both wanted him here and feared his presence. His bold offer in the park and her glimpse behind his stoicism had unnerved her deeply.

She craved him. She might be elderly in Julia's eyes, but Mary was still a strong, healthy woman with strong, healthy appetites.

One reason she'd decided to meet Dougal in London for Christmas this year was because seeing Egan, Zarabeth, and their new son so happy in Scotland too sharply reminded her of her own loneliness. She was very glad for them and loved her tiny nephew, and Egan never made Mary feel that Castle MacDonald was not her home.

But Mary needed more. Her brief affair with an Englishman last year in Edinburgh had been a desperate need to satisfy bodily desire, and had left her feeling colder than ever.

She knew she'd not find coldness with Valentin. He had a fighting man's body—the muscles she had caressed in the park yesterday had been hard and formidable. She'd seen him bare, had stood against him, had shared with him the deep kisses of lovers. Mary's body throbbed with need for him, and what was more—she could love him. She was certain she already did.

She tried to distract herself from thoughts of

Valentin by watching the duchess roam the house, supervising the unpacking and the Christmas decorating. Mary didn't believe for a moment that Sir John Lincolnbury would deliberately involve himself in spying, but Valentin's speculation made Mary wonder. Why *did* the ambassador and dear Duchess Mina take so much interest in Julia and her father? Simple friendliness? Or something more?

Mary shook herself out of her thoughts. She was becoming as conspiracy-minded as Valentin.

The duchess closely watched the English servants who hung ribbons and greens about the house, asking questions at every turn. They would not put up holly yet, Julia told her. It was bad luck to have it in the house before Christmas Day, which Duchess Mina found delightfully superstitious.

They ate an informal luncheon, during which Julia and Duchess Mina chattered like old friends. No one mentioned overthrowing Prince Damien or passing secrets to King George or assassinating anyone. All very harmless.

When the afternoon reached its brightest point, Duchess Mina insisted that the skating party go forward.

"Of course you will skate, Mrs. Cameron," the duchess said when Mary expressed the desire to remain on the canvas-covered bench at the pond's edge and watch. "We all must. Do not ruin my fun."

"Skate with me, Aunt Mary," Julia cried, already on the ice. "You must hold my hand so I do not fall too often."

Resigned, Mary let a Nvengarian footman who doubled as one of the duchess' bodyguards help her strap blades to her flat-soled boots. She hoped she'd not end up on her backside every few feet. Her true reason for not wanting to skate was that she hadn't in years, not since Dougal had been a boy.

The Nvengarian man helped guide her onto the ice, then gave her a slight push when Mary nodded at him to do so. She rocked her body to gain her balance, then tentatively glided out her right foot.

The world spun around her, and she sat down sharply on the ice, legs splayed in front of her. Julia put her hands over her mouth to hide her giggles. The duchess laughed openly then glided across the pond with the ease of long practice.

"You will grow used to it, Mrs. Cameron," Duchess Mina called. "We skate all the time back home."

"I am pleased to hear it," Mary muttered.

Julia helped Mary to her feet. The girl linked arms with her after Mary regained her balance, and they skated slowly after the more competent duchess. The pond curved to the right, angling behind a thicket of trees, but the butler had indicated that the surface closest to where they'd entered was the safest.

"Oh, look," Duchess Mina cried after they'd skated about a quarter of an hour, Mina showing off how gracefully she moved on the ice. "Our gentlemen have arrived. How splendid."

She spun with a flourish, finishing with a pose to greet the men moving along the path from the house. *Pride goeth before a fall,* Mary thought in annoyance. The duchess, however, remained upright.

The train of male figures headed down the muddy and snowy slope—the ambassador, Valentin, and Sir John, followed by Nvengarian servants. The animal in Valentin was evident as he effortlessly navigated the slippery path. The others picked their way carefully, but Valentin moved with unselfconscious grace.

Julia pulled Mary toward the shore and called out to Valentin. "Do come and skate with Aunt Mary, Baron Valentin. She's already fallen once."

Mary flushed. Valentin sent her a ghost of a smile, and Mary's heart turned inside out. Valentin's rare smile was like a gift just for her.

The gentlemen stopped at the bench to don skates, then came onto the ice. Sir John moved across it remarkably well, but he'd been raised in Westmoreland, which must have plenty of frozen ponds in winter. The ambassador was more awkward, but perhaps his duties in the Council of Dukes didn't allow him much time to skate.

Valentin glided to Mary and took her arm. She didn't trust herself alone with him, but nor did she have enough confidence in her ability to remain upright to push him away. Valentin skimmed her along, and they quickly left the others behind.

"You fell?" His breath hung in the air beside her ear. "Are you all right?"

Mary's face heated. "Fine if slightly bruised. Both my pride and my backside."

Valentin's hand on her arm tightened. "Perhaps we should go inside then."

Mary trusted herself alone inside with him still less. "No, no. I am of hearty Scottish stock, not a wilting weed. I will survive it."

She thought she might not survive Valentin's body against her side, though, or the way his thigh brushed hers with every gliding step. She took a long breath, trying to cool herself with the frigid air.

Valentin held her easily as they skated onward, his balance ensuring hers. "What have you discovered from the duchess?"

His mission. Of course. Mary let her voice take a light tone. "That her favorite English Christmas customs are those that might involve men losing their trousers."

Valentin's half smile returned, and Mary decided she should cease joking. She would melt right through the ice if he kept smiling at her like that.

"Jesting aside, she seems harmless," Mary said. "We have unpacked, and Duchess Mina has made plans to skate, light the Yule log, and carry a wassail bowl about to the neighbors. She likes the idea of kissing under the mistletoe, so she has ordered it hung everywhere. Beware of that when you enter the house."

"Hmm." Valentin's brow furrowed, as though he tried to decipher what sort of code Yule logs, mistletoe, and wassail might mean.

"The duchess has so far *not* pumped Julia about her father's business, nor tried to pry English secrets out of her, nor confessed a desire to overthrow the Nvengarian government," Mary went on. "Either she is very careful, or she is innocent. I cannot believe she'd know *nothing* of her husband's involvement in insidious plots."

Valentin rumbled, "Grand Duke Alexander is never wrong."

"Perhaps he isn't, but I do not believe the avenue of danger is through the duchess."

"That may be," Valentin conceded. "But please, keep watching her."

Mary sighed. "I'm not comfortable spying on my friends. I know you grew up in a country full of mad political conspiracies, but I had a fairly normal childhood in a Scottish castle. That is, if you consider being the only girl among a pack of half-crazed

Highland males normal. True, I had to deal with feuds within my own family, but those weren't secret." She broke off under Valentin's unnerving stare. His blue eyes were quiet as he focused all his attention on her. "What is it?" she asked, suppressing a shiver.

"Nothing," he said, his voice low. "I like to watch your lips when you speak."

Mary flushed from the tips of her toes to the roots of her hair. Very well, perhaps he was not focused *only* on his mission. His very rapt attention made her feel like a giddy debutante. "We are skating far from the others," she said breathlessly.

"I know." Valentin's grip on her arm was steadying and warm. "I do not wish them to hear what we are saying."

Because he wanted to talk about his mission, or because he wanted to again say things he'd said yesterday? *I want you as my lover. To give you all that the word means.*

Mary's imagination spun with images of Valentin coming to her bed, his clothing gone, he pulling back covers to put caressing hands on her flesh. Leaning to kiss her, to whisper that he loved her, before he stretched his body over hers and slid inside her, making her complete.

Mary cleared her throat, fire in her veins. She tried to speak normally, but the words were hoarse from her dry throat. "It might be dangerous to go too far. The English servants say we should stay near the banks."

Valentin moved with her around the bend behind the trees then pulled Mary to a halt. The thicket of leafless branches tangled on the bank above them, shielding them from the others.

Valentin tapped the ice with his skate blade. "It is fine here. The water is shallow and frozen hard."

"Have you been out here before?" Mary asked, still shaking from her vision. "I presume so if you are familiar with the depth of the pond."

"I am familiar with ponds in general. We skate often in Nvengaria." Valentin shrugged. "The winters are cold and long so we enjoy whatever we can from them."

She slanted him a look. "When you are trying to convince a lady to come to Nvengaria with you, you ought not to mention long, cold winters. Although I confess winters can be bleak in northern Scotland. I spend most of them in Edinburgh. Or London."

Mary half hoped Valentin would say something about ways they could keep themselves warm through the long winters, but his next words stunned her.

"I have decided to stop trying to persuade you to come to Nvengaria."

Mary went cold, her intake of breath nearly choking her. At the same time, beads of sweat broke out on her brow. "You have, have you?" The words were faint, not defiant as they were meant to be.

"I do not have the gift of persuasion." Valentin slid his hands under her elbows, his grip solid. The look in his blue eyes was not one of a man defeated, however. He looked determined, nearly triumphant, as though he knew he'd already won. "But I do believe in the magic of my people."

"Magic?" Mary repeated in a choked voice. "What do you mean?"

"Today is the winter solstice, the Longest Night. It is said among the logosh that the person you stay with on the Longest Night will remain in your life—

always."

"Are you saying you wish to spend the night with me?" Mary's voice cracked. "You know that is a highly improper suggestion, even to a widowed lady." She didn't mind the suggestion in the least, but she felt obligated to point this out.

"It is why I led you from the others." Valentin leaned to her, his warmth like a blanket. "I want to lie with you, Mary. I have since the day I woke up in Scotland to see you leaning over my bed."

Mary swallowed nervously. "You were ill. I was tending you."

"Yes." The word expanded, slow and rich. "Your hair was mussed, your dress loose, and you smelled like heaven."

Mary's reserve was melting like snow before a summer wind. "I am Julia's chaperone," she tried. "My behavior must be impeccable."

"I am logosh." Valentin's focus returned to her, sharp and honed, the eyes of a wolf. "I know how to come to you without the others knowing."

Mary drew a shaky breath. They swayed a little on the ice, Mary's foot slipping. Valentin's firm hands moved to her back, catching her in his embrace.

It felt good to be held. Mary dearly loved her son and her brother, and Zarabeth and the new baby. But that did not mean her loneliness did not make itself felt.

Mary wanted to be caressed, kissed, told she was desirable. In her world, she was supposed to admit her youth was gone and resign herself to being a widow, a doting mother, a chaperone. No longer wanted by men.

She knew in her heart that this was a lie. Mary

longed for a man's touch, and Valentin, eight years her junior, was gazing at her as though he thought her the most beautiful woman in the world.

If she let him, Valentin would pull her into his strange life, taking her far away from all she knew. In return Mary would have Valentin, with his beautiful eyes, velvet voice, and powerful body. Hers for always.

"I don't know what to do," Mary whispered, a difficult admission.

Valentin's lips moved from the line of her hair to her cheek. "I will come to you, tonight."

Mary touched his face, liking the hardness of his jaw under her glove, the rasp of whiskers catching on the kid leather. He was powerful, handsome, and his warmth under her touch made her heart pound.

"Very well," she heard herself say.

Valentin kissed her then, his mouth commanding. Mary balled her hands on his chest, feeling his heart beating rapidly beneath them.

He tasted raw and wild, like the winter afternoon. He didn't belong in this tame English countryside, with its neat hedgerows and formal gardens that shut out the common people. He fit with the Scottish Highlands, its rugged mountains and cold, dangerous seas.

Mary dug her fingers into his coat, pulling him closer. This wasn't casual for him, she realized. He was as lonely as she was. She wondered if he'd be as formidable in bed as she imagined, and longed to find out.

The quiet moment was shattered by the sharp sound of a pistol shot. Then came the screams of Julia and the duchess, the startled shout of Sir John.

Valentin yanked himself from Mary, and she slid

backward without impediment across the ice. By the time she stopped herself, Valentin was already off the pond and tearing free from his clothes.

Mary skated as fast as she dared to the bank and pulled herself onto firm ground.

Valentin's boots and coat fell empty to the mud beneath the trees. Mary grabbed a branch to steady herself and watched a huge black wolf sprint across the park toward the woods beyond.

Chapter Six

JULIA WOULDN'T CEASE SCREAMING. Mary yanked the skates from her boots and hurried around the snowy banks to the path and bench.

Ambassador Rudolfo lay on his back on the ice, a pool of blood under him, his wife on her knees at his side. Sir John had his hands to his mouth, eyes wide in horror, and Julia stood beside him, shrieking.

The duchess had taken her husband's head into her lap and was parting his clothes to feel his chest. Mary halted on the bank, her heart pounding in fear.

"He's alive," the duchess said crisply, looking up at Mary. "Wounded in the shoulder."

Mary released a breath of relief then let her efficient persona take over. She turned to the servants hurrying down from the house and addressed them in a commanding tone.

"Quickly, carry the ambassador to the house and to his bedroom. *You,* fetch blankets, tell Cook to boil water, and find my box of remedies. Tell the butler to fetch the nearest doctor. Hurry." Mary turned back to the pond as the servants, both Nvengarian and English, rushed to obey her. "Julia, for heaven's sake, stop screaming. The ambassador is not dead."

"But the bullet," Julia sobbed. "It went right past my cheek."

Mary seethed at Nvengarian politics, which did not care if it hurt innocents in its wake. "Come over here to me. I'll take care of you. Everything will be all right."

"Where is Baron Valentin?" Sir John demanded. "He was with you, Mrs. Cameron. Where did he go?"

Mary extemporized. "He ran to find out who was doing the shooting. Do come here, Julia. You are in the way."

As she'd hoped, her sharp tone cut through Julia's hysteria. The girl skated to the bank and climbed out, her eyes wide.

"I thought I saw a wolf, Aunt Mary. An enormous black wolf."

"What absolute nonsense." Mary wrapped her arm around Julia and sat her on the bench to remove her skates. "You saw someone's dog running loose, is all. There are no wolves in this part of England. Not these days."

"But why would someone shoot at us?" Julia bleated. "Are they trying to kill us?"

Mary quickly unbuckled Julia's skates and pulled them off. "I am certain they were stray shots from a shooting party. Foolish city folk going after grouse in entirely the wrong place. Baron Valentin will stop them."

Duchess Mina gave Mary a level look as she followed the footmen carrying her husband. She knew quite well that the shots had been deliberate.

What did not make sense to Mary was why the *ambassador*, suspected by Grand Duke Alexander of plotting against Prince Damien, would be an assassin's target. Perhaps the Grand Duke had sent the assassin himself, not wanting to wait until Valentin finished his investigation. But would Alexander deliberately endanger Valentin or Mary or innocent Julia in the attempt? She did not think so.

Or perhaps these shooters were from a different group altogether. The ambassador could have more enemies than Grand Duke Alexander. Nvengaria was rife with plots.

At least Mary knew Valentin hadn't shot the ambassador. He'd been at her side when the gun had been fired.

Her heart pumped faster as she thought of Valentin charging into the woods to hunt the hunters. As a logosh, Valentin possessed strength beyond an ordinary man's, but these men had weapons.

With much fuss — and sobbing from Julia — Duke Rudolfo was carried into the house and up the stairs to his bedroom. He woke as the footmen bore him into his bedchamber, pressed his hand to his wound, and groaned.

Mary assumed she'd end up doing most of the nursing, but Duchess Mina proved unexpectedly competent. Mary helped her put the ambassador to bed and bathe his wound, but the duchess firmly took charge.

The doctor, a country man of round face and genial speech who was also a surgeon, arrived soon after that. He gave Rudolfo a good dose of laudanum then pried open his shoulder and probed for the bullet.

The duchess did have to leave the room then, calling for smelling salts. The other servants turned green and sidled off, and it was Mary who held the bowl to receive the bloody bullet.

She did so without squeamishness. Growing up in a household of boisterous Scotsmen, Mary had become used to helping set broken bones and patching up wounds, even extracting stray bullets from sheepish men. This was all quite familiar.

Mary chafed at the delay, however, because she wanted to retrieve Valentin's clothes from the woods before anyone found them. Valentin himself had not been seen or heard from since the shooting.

"This one is easy," the doctor said cheerfully as the round bullet clinked into the bowl. "I've wrenched out many a ball lodged right into the bone when I was a surgeon on the Peninsula. Sawed off my share of legs too. This is the most interesting wound I've tended since I became a country doctor, except for the poor lad gored by one of his oxen two summers ago."

Mary offered no comment. She wiped away blood while the army surgeon turned doctor sewed the wound shut, then she helped him make the ambassador comfortable.

The sun slid behind the horizon as the doctor packed up and left, the Longest Night beginning. Mary callously handed the bowl and bullet to the nearest footman, suggesting he clean the bullet and offer it to the ambassador as a souvenir. Then she hastened down the stairs to see the doctor out, hoping to slip away and fetch Valentin's discarded clothes.

Too late.

The ambassador's valet, a small, fastidious Nvengarian who'd excused himself during the doctor's work, came in the front door carrying Valentin's clothing and boots.

Mary moved to intercept him. "I will take those."

"Isn't that Baron Valentin's coat?" Julia came charging out of the drawing room with her father on her heels. "Where is Baron Valentin?"

"Where did you find 'em?" Sir John asked. He touched the coat as the valet handed it to Mary.

The valet only had a smattering of English. "By the frozen water," he managed.

"Strange place for the fellow to disrobe, eh?"

"He didn't disrobe, Papa. The wolf took him." Julia clapped her hands to her cheeks. "Oh dear heaven, the wolf's eaten Baron Valentin!"

Sir John looked shocked, the valet confused. Mary snatched the boots. "Julia, please. If you examine these clothes you will see that they are quite whole. What wolf undresses his dinner before eating it?"

"Oh." Julia looked doubtful. "But why on earth did the baron leave his clothes near the pond? How can he run about without them?"

"Perhaps somebody stole 'em," Sir John suggested. "Shoved them down there, planning to fetch them later. Baron Valentin can tell us if he has any missing. Where *is* the fellow, by the way?"

"Still trying to discover who shot the ambassador, I'd imagine." Mary turned away to the stairs.

"Oh, that chappie wasn't shooting at the ambassador," Sir John said in his ingenuous voice. "He was shooting at me."

Mary swung around in surprise. "At you, John? Why on earth should someone shoot at you?"

"No idea, my dear," Sir John answered without

worry. "But Duke Rudolfo pushed me out of the way and took the bullet himself." He puffed out his chest. "Damned decent of him, I'd say. Good fellow, that ambassador, even if he is foreign."

* * *

THE WOLF APPROACHED THE HOUSE under cover of darkness, sensing the warmth within. The mansion was a bulk of shadow in deeper darkness, the lower floor black, with only a few lights in the upper floors.

The strange ditch the English called a *ha-ha* might keep out a wandering tramp, but to a nimble animal it presented no barrier. Valentin easily leapt the ditch and scrambled down the bank to the shadows of the house.

On the back wall, which faced the pond, two square windows showed candlelight. The wolf knew the window on the far left was the ambassador's bedroom, the one on the far right, Mary's.

Nvengarians considered logosh demons. Logosh regarded themselves as simply logosh — beings who had inhabited the Nvengarian mountains for eons. They were shape-shifters, able to take animal, demon, or human form as they chose.

Valentin was only half logosh, and he'd always found shifting painful. He clenched his teeth as he forced his wolf limbs to change to the demon's. Fur became skin, paws became claws, and his thighs thickened with logosh muscle. All creatures but logosh considered the logosh's demon form hideous, but in it, Valentin could climb.

He moved swiftly and noiselessly up the wall to the lighted window and peered into what must be Mary's dressing room. An open wardrobe showing neat rows of garments stood next to an armless chaise. At the dressing table, ribbons had been sorted tidily, as had her cosmetics and jewelry. Not one stray glove, hat, or handkerchief rested on any piece of furniture. The pristine neatness of it made him want to smile.

Mary leaned over the washbasin near the window, scooping water from her hands to her face. She'd slid her bodice from her torso, letting the fabric hang limply from her waist. The short corset and her chemise beneath were splotched with water.

Valentin hooked his claw around the edge of the casement and pulled, surprised when the window opened easily. Mary had left it unlatched, just as she hadn't drawn the curtains. She likely thought no one would see her in this high window, with plenty of woods and fields between her and the house in the next valley.

He'd meant to be silent, but at the window's slight squeak, Mary raised her head and looked around. She did nothing—no scream or startled cry came from her, no fear. She watched silently, her eyes wide, her hands dripping, while a logosh climbed into her chamber.

"I do hope that's you, Valentin," she said, her voice faint. "Or is there another logosh running about the place?"

Valentin willed his body to become human again. His fingers ached as they moved from claw to human flesh, then his face flattened, his hair grew warm on his head, and his back straightened. Valentin growled, fisting his hands, willing the pain to stop.

Mary stepped past him to close and latch the window. She jerked the heavy drape across it, and when she turned around again, he moved to her, standing close.

"What happened to you?" Mary whispered. Her

dark eyes held worry. "What did you find?"

Not now. Valentin was naked, he hurt, and he needed her. He wrapped his arms around her, jerked her close, and slanted a kiss across her mouth.

Mary made a protesting noise in her throat, but then she sagged against him, holding on to him as tightly as he clung to her. Valentin unraveled her coiled hair, pulling it loose, burying his hands in it. He tasted the water from the basin on her lips, mingling with the sweetness of *her*.

This was why Valentin had returned to Britain, to find Mary, to kiss her, to love her. To persuade her to come home with him. This time he would not leave without her.

He spread kisses down her neck to where her breasts swelled from her chemise. Mary cradled him against her, fingers furrowing his hair. He tugged at the laces of her corset, loosening them and spreading the corset open with his broad hand.

Valentin raised his head to kiss her lips again. "Let me love you, Mary."

"Yes." The word was a gasp. "My bedchamber …"

Valentin was too impatient to seek a bed. He pulled the laces from her stays and let the corset fall, unbuttoned her chemise and pushed it down as well. He caught her unfettered breasts in his hands—they were full and round, the breasts of a beautiful woman. He licked between them, loving her scalding heat.

Mary unhooked her skirts and petticoat and pushed them down her hips. Her chemise floated downward with them, fabric puddling on the floor. Her stocking-clad calves brushed Valentin's legs, but otherwise, she was as bare as he.

She leaned into him as he moved his hand down the back of her thigh. "I wish I could be young and beautiful for you," she said softly.

What was she talking about? Valentin gently turned her around to face her mirror, which put her backside against the swell of his cock. "You are the most beautiful woman I have ever known," he said and nipped her ear. "Look at yourself."

The mirror reflected them together, her pale body wrapped in his darker limbs. Valentin's large hand rested on her breast, wisps of her long hair curling around his fingers. He slid his hand down her abdomen to the dark tuft between her thighs, smiling when he found it pleasingly damp.

"Your body is my heaven." Valentin touched each part of her as he spoke. "Your thighs have strength, your hips are smooth, your breasts ..." He returned his hand to the heat beneath them. Her nipples were dark, tight points he wanted to suckle. "I love your breasts."

Mary traced her lower abdomen, which was softly rounded. "I've had a husband and a lover, and I have a grown son."

Valentin rolled her nipple between finger and thumb. "Why should these things make you less beautiful?"

"Because you are young and strong, and ... heartbreakingly handsome. You should be with a young woman, one who can give you a family." She smiled sadly. "I'm rather past it."

"Past it?" English expressions baffled him.

"You make me feel like a giddy girl, but I know how old I am."

Valentin's blue gaze caught her brown one in the mirror. "My body wants yours, can you not feel?" He shifted the ridge of his arousal until it slid firmly between her buttocks. "I find you desirable, or I would not ache for you so much."

Mary swallowed. "Lust of the moment is not the same thing."

For answer, Valentin turned her around again and kissed her hard on the mouth. He pulled her up into him, tasting her once more, showing her what he thought of her words.

When he lifted from the kiss, Mary stared at him, her lips parted and red. With a growl, Valentin swept her into his arms and carried her to the narrow chaise. He deposited her there, his body pressing Mary's down. He gazed at her, face to face, then drew back to study the whole of her, hungrily taking her in.

Valentin splayed his hand across her abdomen. "Is *past it* the English way of saying you have no interest in pleasures of the flesh?"

Mary's brows went up, but she smiled shakily. "No, it is the English way of saying I no longer *should* have interest in pleasures of the flesh."

"Do you mean you take no interest in this?" Valentin slid his hand down to dip between her legs. He cupped her, fingers brushing the heat he found. "Or this?" He slid his first two fingers inside her.

Mary inhaled sharply, liquid heat pouring over his hand. "No. No interest at all." Her words were barely coherent.

Valentin eased his fingers from her and raised them to his lips.

Did anything taste better than a woman aroused? Did any woman taste better than Mary? It could not be so.

Valentin leaned down and nuzzled her neck, then

kissed between her breasts, working his way down to the indentation of her navel. He nipped her belly where she'd touched as she watched herself in the mirror, then at last put his mouth where his fingers had been.

Bliss. He suckled her, surrounded by her incredible scent. *Love you, Mary. Gods, how I love you.*

"Valentin …" The whisper was full of longing.

Now. Valentin rolled to his feet and lifted Mary into his arms again. Swiftly he sat down in the middle of the chaise, pulling Mary on top of him. He showed her how to wrap her legs around him — *just like that* — so that he could slide into her warm, pliant body.

She was tight and beautiful, enveloping him with arms and legs, her breasts soft against his chest. Mary made warm noises in her throat, her lips on his forehead, his hair, his brow. Valentin gripped her hips and rocked up into her.

The beast in him roared. He'd found his mate, the true match to his soul. He would make her understand that they belonged together, that he was not leaving this place without her.

Mary's teeth scraped his earlobe, her wanting turning as furious as his own. The sharp little pain made him move faster, sliding in, *in*. She was his home, his resting place, the woman who could soothe his hurts. She was a lush armful, her long hair tumbling between them and warming him.

"Valentin," she said in a ragged whisper. "I …"

He cupped her face in his hands, their bodies moving together. "What?" He willed her to say the words he wanted to hear.

Mary shook her head, her hair brushing his face. "Love me," she pleaded. "Just love me."

Valentin leaned back, pulling her down harder onto him. He wanted to tell her what he felt, how much he needed her, but his command of English fled him. He said the words in Nvengarian, that he loved her, he wanted her, for now, for always.

He felt her body shudder. Mary opened her eyes in surprise, as though she'd never broken in climax before. Valentin feared for a moment that she'd fight it, Mary who loved control.

Then she laughed. She dropped her head back, her glorious hair tumbling down her back. Her body rocked as she dragged everything from him into herself.

Valentin's excitement tipped him over the edge. They moved together, gripping, loving, gasping, she so tight on him that he couldn't stop his shout of pleasure.

Mary lifted her head and gazed at him, the brown of her eyes coffee-dark. Valentin wanted her to look at him like that for the rest of his life.

"Mary ..." He spoke a few more words in Nvengarian, then halted, forcing himself to repeat them in English. "You are mine. Forever. Say it is true."

Mary closed her eyes. She shook her head as she held him, and Valentin gave up, groaning as he released his seed. He collapsed to the cushions with Mary tangled around him, breathing like a drowning man who at last finds shore.

Chapter Seven

MARY WOKE IN THE MORNING with Valentin in her bed. She opened her eyes to find herself nose-to-nose with him, his blue irises wide with that *otherness* he had.

Without dismay, Valentin smiled. His face was creased from the pillows, his hair pleasantly rumpled. He was so handsome, loving, and desirable, that Mary tightened in sudden panic.

"Will it come true, do you think?" he asked softly.

She blinked. "Will what come true?" She couldn't remember anything they'd discussed before he'd come to her through her window last night, to hold her, kiss her …

Valentin lifted a curl from her face, his strong touch gentled. "The legend of the Longest Night. Will the lady I spent it with be with me for the rest of my life?"

Mary struggled to sit up. "Not if someone finds you in bed with me. I'll be utterly disgraced."

"I locked the door. And what if they do discover us? Do you care so much what these English people think of you?"

She didn't, not at this moment. Mary put her hand to her hair, finding it warm and tangled. "Some of the people are Nvengarian. Your people."

"Who would not find it surprising that I want to be with you." Valentin smiled the heart-melting smile that made anything he said sound reasonable. "If you are forced to flee the country, you can always come home with me."

Mary wanted to laugh with him, but her heart beat faster. If a maid did try to come in to stir the fire and found her here—she would be talked about, and Julia could be caught in the gossip. She'd be pointed at as the young lady with the scandalous chaperone, her reputation speculated about as well. Not fair, but that was the way of the world.

"We shouldn't joke," Mary said quickly.

"No? Come home with me anyway, Mary. It is nothing to be ashamed of."

"Perhaps not in your world, but mine is a different place," she said in worry. "If we are discovered, I will be the entertainment of the *ton*— talked about, laughed at. The matron who fell for the young, handsome foreigner with the enticing eyes."

A crease appeared between Valentin's brows. "Are you so ashamed then? Of what we did? Of who I am?"

"Of course not!" Mary's anger rose—both at the easily shocked English and the altogether too-permissive Nvengarians. She was Scottish, neither one, but she felt pinched between the two worlds. She wondered if Egan had felt like this when he moved from Scotland to Nvengaria and back again.

No, Egan did as he pleased and damned what everyone else thought. Egan had traveled the world, playing the Mad Highlander, entertaining everyone he met. Mary had always wished for her brother's gift of easy charm. Perhaps then she'd be able to fall into Valentin's arms and let him take her away from her old life and everything she knew.

The trouble was, she didn't hate her old life. Her marriage had been a failure, and now she was lonely, but she had Dougal, her family and friends, and her home at Castle MacDonald. There was nothing better in her opinion than the laughter that filled Castle MacDonald to its rafters. Even Sir John and Julia were ties to her childhood, to a friend she'd talked with and giggled with—the two of them had once run away to Edinburgh to shop without permission, feeling themselves wicked and daring.

Mary did not want to fling away the happy parts of her life for Valentin, but neither did she want to sacrifice being with Valentin for them. Valentin seemed to think that waltzing off to the eastern edge of Europe at a moment's notice was nothing difficult. But Nvengaria was the end of civilization as far as Mary was concerned.

Valentin was watching her with his intense blue eyes, knowing he hadn't won, not yet. "I'll not give up, Mary."

Before she could answer, Valentin slid his arms around her and pulled her down to him.

Mary went all too willingly. She let him kiss her, let his body heat hers. She never felt so good as when he touched her. Valentin's returning smile told him he knew it, drat him.

Valentin kissed her lips and her face as he gently rolled her over into the pillows. Mary wanted to tell him that he really should go before someone discovered him there. But she couldn't speak as Valentin pressed her into the bed with his warm weight and loved her all over again.

* * *

VALENTIN DESCENDED TO THE BREAKFAST ROOM much later to find the rest of the household already at table, Mary included, looking neat and efficient as ever. Even Duke Rudolfo had risen from his bed, one arm in a sling, and was eating buttered toast with his good hand.

Valentin had made himself leave Mary after their enjoyment this morning, to return stealthily to his own chamber to bathe and dress. He felt buoyant and good, the memory of Mary beneath him imprinted firmly on his body. He both liked the feeling and knew it would distract him all day, until he could love her again.

The breakfast room was one of light and glass. The floor-to-ceiling windows facing the frozen pond let in weak winter sunlight, and a fire in the hearth added to the coziness. Not the best room to linger in, Valentin reflected as he gathered food from the sideboard, if one feared sharpshooters.

Mary had taken little on her plate, but Julia's was piled high with eggs, sausages, ham, and toast, as was her father's. Duchess Mina pushed the remains of her breakfast aside and sipped chocolate from a dainty cup.

"I still believe the shots were fired at me," Sir John was saying as Valentin seated himself across the table from Mary.

Valentin couldn't keep his gaze from Mary, but she only gave him a polite nod as though they were acquaintances, no more. The pretense made Valentin want to laugh. Mary was expert at deception.

"I make a great deal of money in the City," Sir John droned on in his odd accent. "Perhaps someone wants to eliminate m' wealth by eliminating me." He chortled.

"Oh, Papa, do not laugh," Julia cried. "It frightened me so."

Ambassador Rudolfo cleared his throat. "I am not certain, Sir John. I heard the shots and pushed you down to the ice, because you were nearest to me. He must have been firing at me. Nvengarians are notorious for eliminating each other, as you say. Perhaps I have angered a rival."

"It is safer these days in Nvengaria," Duchess Mina pointed out after another sip of chocolate. "Perhaps you should resign your post, Rudolfo, and we will return home and have done with politics."

Rudolfo gave her a fond look. "No, my dear, I will not run away because of a few bullets. All will be well."

"There were two men," Valentin broke in.

At this abrupt announcement, everyone jerked their attention to him as though they'd forgotten his presence. Julia and her father halted in mid-chew, and the duchess peered at him over the rim of her cup. Only Mary would not look directly at him.

"I investigated the area last night," Valentin said, trying not to be unnerved by their stares. "Two men stood in the trees, on the rise there." He pointed out the window to high ground beyond the pond's icy sheet. "They were gone by then, but I found evidence of them. They drank whisky to keep warm and dropped the flask when it was empty. They were Englishmen, not Nvengarian."

Sir John swallowed noisily. "Good Lord, how the

devil d'ye know that?"

Valentin couldn't very well tell him that his wolf had smelled that they were English, not Scottish, or Irish, or of any other people. The inhabitants of England had their own peculiar scent, as did Nvengarians.

"They wore English-made boots," he improvised. "The prints are different." That, at least, was true.

"That's clever of you," Sir John said in an admiring voice. "But how d'ye know they weren't Nvengarians in English suits?"

The ambassador answered before Valentin could think of a plausible reason. "Nvengarians do not like to wear English clothes. And when Nvengarians assassinate, they stand up and do it—they don't skulk behind trees and shoot when innocent people are about."

"Good heavens, they might have hit *me*," Julia said.

"Is that where you were all night, Valentin?" Duke Rudolfo asked. "Miss Lincolnbury thought you'd been devoured by wolves." He chuckled, then winced as his shoulder moved with his laugh.

"*I* told her that was nonsense," Mary said in a firm voice.

"I was investigating," Valentin said. "I did not see a wolf."

The ambassador gingerly touched his coat where the bandage bulged beneath it. "The butler told me another strange tale this morning. He swore he saw a monstrous creature prowling outside the house late in the night. It had the face of the devil, he said."

Valentin didn't change expression. "I saw nothing of that, either."

He flicked his gaze at Mary, but she went on

calmly eating, a faint tinge of pink on her cheeks.

The duchess clicked her cup to her saucer. "Do stop pushing at your wound, Rudolfo. You'll open it again. Wolves and monsters notwithstanding, my English country Christmas must continue. We had to postpone the Yule log and the wassail yesterday, but today, we shall do all this."

"Perhaps we should not ride about with the wassail bowl," Mary said. "We will have to travel on open roads, and the men with the guns might try again."

The duchess waved that away. "We will go in a large party with guards and be perfectly well. Rudolfo will stay home, watched by his own bodyguards, of course."

Mary at last let her gaze meet Valentin's, her exasperation evident. Valentin gave her a little smile, and his heartbeat quickened when she gave him a hint of smile in return.

Her smallest gesture stirred his blood. Valentin wanted to finish with this business quickly so he could return his attention to convincing Mary to come home with him. His body heated as he remembered the warmth of her skin against his, her sweet cries as he loved her.

Valentin wanted to hold her in the night for the rest of his life. His smile turned determined, and Mary flushed and hurriedly looked away.

* * *

"I AM PLEASED BARON VALENTIN STAYED behind today," Duchess Mina said as she rode next to Mary in the stuffy traveling coach.

Another carriage bearing Julia and her father and two English servants with the wassail bowl followed. Four Nvengarian bodyguards rode nearby, but for some reason Mary did not feel protected. Valentin and two more bodyguards had remained at the house with Duke Rudolfo while Duchess Mina resolutely went on with her wassailing party.

Mary could not agree it was good that Valentin had stayed behind. She wanted Valentin beside her, needed him next to her every moment.

She'd told him she did not want to not leave for Nvengaria with him, but her heart knew the lie. Mary craved to be with him day and night forever. Her entire body was loose from their loving this morning, and a warm core burned inside her.

As the carriages wound through the countryside under clear, white-blue skies, Mary sensed eyes watching them. The eerie feeling made her shiver, and the cold wind buffeting the carriage did not help.

Duchess Mina leaned to Mary, her exotic perfume cloying. "I did not like to say so in front of the others, my dear, but I believe it was Valentin himself who fired those shots at my husband."

Mary opened her mouth to explain that Valentin couldn't have—she'd been talking to him when they'd heard the pistol, when she remembered that no, she'd been standing in Valentin's arms, kissing him. Her face burned.

She closed her mouth again and contrived to look surprised. "Good heavens, why would you think so?"

"I can not blame him," Duchess Mina went on sadly. "Poor Valentin has had a difficult life, and he's never forgiven Rudolfo."

Mary stopped, now truly puzzled. "The ambassador? Forgiven him for what?"

"He did not tell you this?" Mina looked

astonished and also distressed. "Rudolfo was *there*, my dear. On the day the Imperial Prince called on poor Sophie."

Mary's breath quickened—the ambassador had known? Hadn't done anything to stop it? Anger built inside her. "Good heavens," was all she could trust herself to say.

"Yes." Mina nodded, unhappy. "Rudolfo was in the hunting party when it fetched up at Valentin's estate. Everything was in great disrepair, Rudolfo told me, because years before that, Valentin's father had done something to offend the Imperial Prince. I've never discovered what—probably he'd done nothing at all, and the prince invented the tale in order to take his money. Valentin's father lost all his wealth and died a broken man." The duchess shook her head as she looked out at the bare, dead trees that lined the fields.

She obviously did not plan to continue, so Mary seized her hands. "Please tell me what happened, Mina. I need to know."

Mina turned back to her, the pain in her eyes deep. "It is so a sad story, Mrs. Cameron. When the hunters arrived at the house and the Imperial Prince ascertained that Sophie was alone, he sent his men off to pen up the servants and do what they liked with them. Then the Imperial Prince took Sophie into a bedchamber and locked the door. He made Rudolfo stand guard outside. Rudolfo did not know what to do. He was sick at heart."

Mary's own heart flooded with rage. "Well, he ought to have done *something*. Do you mean to say he kicked his heels in the corridor while his prince ravished Valentin's sister in the next room?"

The duchess furrowed her brow. "*Kicked his heels?*

I do not understand."

"An English expression meaning waiting or wasting time. You are avoiding the question. Why did your husband do nothing?"

"Because of me." Duchess Mina sighed. "Rudolfo feared that if he interfered with the prince's wishes it would endanger me and our daughter, who was a debutante at the time. We could not know if the Imperial Prince would mete out the same sentence on our family that he did to Valentin's. He likely would have, unfortunately. It was no idle worry."

Mary balled her gloved fists. "Then Duke Rudolfo ought to have finished off the Imperial Prince then and there. It would not be unusual for Nvengarians—I am told they run each other through on far less provocation. Had *I* been there, I certainly would have taken up a pistol and shot the bloody prince dead."

Duchess Mina smiled suddenly. "Do you know, my dear, I believe you would have. You are a woman of great courage. Luckily Grand Duke Alexander saved us all from the Imperial Prince not long later."

"You believe Alexander poisoned the Imperial Prince?" Mary asked distractedly. "Does anyone know that for certain?"

"Of course not, but we all *know*, if you understand me." Duchess Mina gave her a wise nod. "In any case, Alexander helped drive the prince completely mad, and the man died."

Mary shivered, but she couldn't help feeling some satisfaction at Alexander's methods. Her wild Highlander blood wished she could turn back the clock and rush to Sophie's rescue that day. She'd have told the Imperial Prince what she thought of men like him before she fired her shot.

"But Valentin was not content with the Imperial Prince's death," Duchess Mina continued. "He is obsessed with vengeance. Valentin tried to kill Prince Damien, you know, though he was thwarted from that. He no doubt came with us to England for a chance to punish Rudolfo. Valentin wants revenge on all who were with the Imperial Prince that day."

Mary's head began to ache. She remembered what Valentin had told her at the ball in London—that he'd traveled here at the request of Alexander to spy on Duke Rudolfo. She was certain that some of the ambassador's bodyguards and servants were spying on Valentin and the duke both. Spies on the spies, in the mad confusion of Nvengarian politics.

Mary could clear up some confusion at least. "Valentin did not shoot your husband, Your Grace," she said in a brisk tone. "When the shots were fired, Valentin was with me. We were talking together, screened from view by the trees."

The duchess looked disbelieving. "Why did he not come out with you then? *You* rushed to us right away to see what was the matter, but Valentin disappeared."

"He ran off in the other direction to find the source of the shots." Which was true. There, that should satisfy all the questions.

Duchess Mina smiled archly. "Leaving his clothes behind?"

Mary flushed. "He … "

The duchess patted Mary's knee. "My dear, do not bother to explain. I know you are his lover. I know he stayed in your room last night. Oh, yes, I am not as slow-witted as I seem. I know when a woman loves a man. But please be careful, Mrs. Cameron. Baron Valentin might not have shot the pistol himself, but he could have hired others to do so, you know."

Mary began to argue that in that case, *anyone* could have hired them, but Duchess Mina firmly changed the subject. Mary found herself woodenly answering questions about the differences between English and Scottish Christmas and New Year's customs while they continued to the house of the nearest neighbor.

As they wended down the country lane between cheerful villages, Mary swore she glimpsed a black wolf trailing them, keeping to the fringes of the woods. She watched without drawing attention to the fact, but the wolf never approached and disappeared altogether when they finally returned to the ambassador's house late in the winter-dark evening.

Chapter Eight

VALENTIN SCRAPED THE SKIN OFF HIS HANDS while helping the footmen position the Yule log in the drawing room's huge fireplace that night. The duchess, Julia, and Mary tied ribbons to the branches, and Julia explained they each had to sit on the log at least once, to ensure they'd have luck in the coming year.

Traditionally, the Yule log was to be lit with a branch from the previous year's, but the prior inhabitants of the house apparently hadn't burned one. The duchess made do with a freshly cut sliver from the woodpile, and soon she had everyone coaxing the log to burn.

As soon as it caught, Mary said in her efficient voice that Valentin needed his hands looked after. She bade him go the dining room across the hall, where she joined him after fetching her bag of remedies.

Valentin didn't mind Mary standing close to him,

never noticed the sting on his palms as she dabbed them with a damp cloth scented with calendula and beeswax. The odor of the salve filled his nostrils, and Mary's warm body against to his did dangerous things to his heart.

"I saw you following us," Mary said in a low voice as she worked. "I thought you were to stay with the ambassador while we paraded about the countryside." She bent to study his palm, her hair tickling his nose. "I don't believe any of the others marked that you were near."

Valentin realized that her hair touched his face because he'd instinctively leaned to her. He spoke into her ear. "I followed because I believe Sir John is correct that he was the intended victim."

Mary jerked her head up, nearly colliding with him. "Truly? Why?"

Valentin liked having her face an inch from his. "Perhaps he knows something he should not. Perhaps he is a go-between someone fears, a go-between who needs to be removed."

"Removed?" Mary's brows rose. "You mean *killed*, don't you? Good grief, Sir John was married to my dearest friend. I can't let him be *removed*. What would become of Julia?"

"This is why I followed you today, to keep Sir John safe. Happily I saw no one to put him or you in danger on your outing."

"Thank heavens for that." Mary resumed wiping his palms. Her ministration was unnecessary—as a logosh, Valentin healed quickly. But he enjoyed how tenderly she nursed him, the lightness of her fingers on his skin.

Mary turned to her remedy box, but Valentin caught her arm. He'd yearned for her all day, could barely contain his patience for the household to go to bed. When things grew quiet tonight, he'd slip into Mary's room, run his hands across her body, and ease every bit of her worry with his kisses.

Mary stepped from his grasp. "The others might come in," she said softly.

"We have the excuse of mistletoe." Valentin pointed at a gray-green ball hanging from a chandelier.

Mary didn't laugh. Her stance, her tension, began to worry him.

"What is it?" he asked, his amusement dying.

She stood silently a moment, her look unhappy. "The duchess told me Duke Rudolfo accompanied the Imperial Prince to your house that day."

Valentin stifled a growl. Damn Duchess Mina's gossiping tongue. Why the woman wished Mary to know these things Valentin couldn't understand.

Mary watched Valentin, willing him to be truthful with her, no matter how much it hurt.

"She is correct," Valentin said, drawing a breath. "Duke Rudolfo was with the prince."

"Why did you not tell me?" Mary asked, brows drawn down.

Valentin closed his fingers on Mary's arm but kept his touch light. "Because I hate to think of that time, that most horrible day of my life. I know Duke Rudolfo could have done nothing to save Sophie. The Imperial Prince would have killed Rudolfo's family in retaliation if he had interfered. I know this. The Imperial Prince was a monster."

Mary's gaze didn't waver. "Duchess Mina fears that you have come here to kill her husband."

Valentin gave a reluctant nod. "And I must, if he proves to be working against Prince Damien."

"Is Duchess Mina right then?" Mary asked. "That you live for vengeance? Is this why you so eagerly agreed to Grand Duke Alexander's assignment?"

Valentin's grip tightened. "I told you why I *so eagerly* agreed to come."

"But you had no idea I'd be in here," Mary said in bewilderment. "It was chance that we were in London at the same time, dragged to the same ball."

"That was simply good fortune." Valentin shook his head. "I agreed to Alexander's task because it took me to England. I had been saving the money to make the journey myself, but I snatched this opportunity. I planned to make my way to Scotland and Castle MacDonald when this business with the ambassador was finished, for good or for ill."

"Oh." Mary looked startled.

Valentin clasped her hands between his, not caring that his palms still stung. "You belong with me, my Mary. I knew it the first time I looked at you. I need you."

Again she stared, needing to understand. "But do I need you?" she asked softly.

She stood so close that her breath touched his skin. She smelled good, warm with perspiration and the salve, and Valentin wanted to drink her in. "I hope that you do."

"Even if you have no wish to marry me?" Her words were barely a breath.

Valentin gripped her hands tighter. "If marriage is what you want, I will work to make it so. My estate is recovering under Prince Damien's rule. It will take time to make it yield enough for you to not be ashamed to be my wife, but I will work hard to bring this about."

Mary gave him an indignant look. "I would never

be ashamed to be your wife. But I must understand you." She leaned closer after a glance out the door to the crowd in the next room. "You say you do not blame Duke Rudolfo for standing by while the Imperial Prince hurt your sister, but how can that be true? I'd be enraged at anyone who didn't keep my son, or Egan, or my sister-in-law—anyone I loved—from harm. At anyone who stood by to save his own skin, in fact."

She was stubbornly proud, his Highland lass. The strength of her people flowed through her, and Valentin loved her for it.

He released her hands. He remembered the impossible rage that had filled him when he'd found Sophie in a tight ball on her bed, too stunned and shocked to even cry. Sophie's maid had told Valentin the tale, every detail. The maid herself had been beaten until she couldn't stand by the Imperial Prince's guards because she'd tried to protect Sophie.

Valentin folded his arms across his chest, closing in on himself. "I was angry with Rudolfo, yes, and I still have that anger—I will not lie. Duke Rudolfo should never have let him touch Sophie. If he'd shot the Imperial Prince that day, I doubt the Council of Dukes would have minded."

"Will you try to kill Rudolfo now?" Mary asked him. "You can make him pay for being a spy and take your revenge at the same time. Two birds with one stone."

He liked her no-nonsense tone—Mary ever saw a thing for what it was. "It is complicated," Valentin answered. "I am angry, yes, but I also have my duty to Damien and Alexander. My personal wishes are no longer important."

Mary gave him an astonished look. "Of course

they are important. You think it is too Nvengarian for me to understand, and you are right. I don't understand. I am too *Scottish* to understand. In my world, the personal is *far* more important. A clan lord would grant you leave if you had to take care of a personal feud before answering his call to arms. He might even help you. That way, he'd know you'd be finished with the business and not distracted."

"I *am* finished," Valentin said in a firm voice.

"Are you? How can I be certain you won't rush off on an unfinished vendetta as soon as you take me home with you? Or that Grand Duke Alexander won't send you to do your 'duty' with another insurrectionist? When will you stop being the dagger hand of Prince Damien and the Grand Duke and simply be Valentin? The man I can love?"

Valentin's wolf growl emerged. "I am not their servant ..."

"Aren't you?" Mary put her hands on her hips. "And yet every time I see you, you are on some assignment for them. I want *you*, Valentin. Not the bodyguard or the spy or the hired assassin. Dear heavens, Alexander expects you to *murder* a man if he turns out not to love Prince Damien."

"Of course he does." Valentin clenched his fists, willing her to understand. "You do not know how dangerous men like Rudolfo can be. If I discover he is working to bring down Prince Damien, Rudolfo will make certain I never report to Nvengaria. He would not hesitate to kill *you*, or your Sir John or even Julia to stop me. In my world, secrets must be kept secret. At all costs."

"Well, it is a bloody inconvenient world, isn't it?" Mary stepped to him, her dark eyes swimming with tears. "I don't think I could live there. I have a son to think of."

"Mary, let me finish this, and then we will speak."

She gave him a sorrowful look. "I want life and love, not death. I will not marry that."

Valentin suppressed a snarl. He'd never been given to demonstrating his rage, always needing to keep the beast inside him at bay. He knew that if he ever gave into that beast and its basic, volatile emotion, he'd become more of a monster than the Imperial Prince had ever been.

"I did not offer marriage," he said. "I told you I could not. Not yet."

"I know. You offered me compromises, conveniences even. That is not what I want."

"What *do* you want, then?"

"I have told you," Mary said.

She wanted certainty—Valentin saw that—and Valentin's entire existence was based on *un*certainty. He was logosh, he was Nvengarian, he was working to regain the trust of Prince Damien and Grand Duke Alexander. He pressed his lips together, his heart a burning lump in his chest.

When Valentin said nothing, Mary kissed the corner of his mouth, picked up her bag of medicine, and walked away from him. Her skirts whispered as she went, her footsteps light as she left the room.

The click of the door closing behind her was the bleakest thing Valentin had ever heard in his life.

* * *

MARY WAS READY TO RUN BACK TO LONDON that very evening, but after a bout of agitated pacing in her bedchamber, she decided to stay.

Leaving would draw attention, plus she would not let herself be such a coward. She would stay and face Valentin and the world, not rush off to lick her wounds and cry into her pillow. She could not justify abandoning Julia or wresting the girl from Hertfordshire when Julia was so enjoying herself. Mary had never seen her this happy before.

Resolved, Mary arrived at the supper table that night in time to hear Duchess Mina reveal more plans for her very English Christmas.

Mary sank to her place in the richly paneled dining room where she'd ministered to Valentin, both relieved and worried to not see Valentin there. He'd gone out, Duke Rudolfo said, to look for the shooters again. Rudolfo was convinced the gunmen had given up and gone away, but Valentin had insisted on checking.

Hunting, Mary amended in her head. She could imagine him moving through the woods and across fields in his wolf form, tracking the shooters, stopping every once in a while to sniff the air. He'd sit still while wind ruffled his fur and moonlight glinted on his sleek black body.

"A mummers play," the duchess interrupted from her end of the table, her shrill voice making Mary jump. "As I was saying to the others, Mrs. Cameron, we'll be the mummers ourselves and invite the neighbors round to see us."

Mary reflected that the neighbors might well have had enough of their foreign visitors trying to be so very English, but she nodded. Julia jiggled in excitement—she *adored* dramatics.

Julia and Duchess Mina conferred on the play in the drawing room after supper, asking for pointers from Mary and Sir John on how to keep everything traditional.

To Mary's dismay, the ambassador announced that he would not be needed in London until after

Boxing Day, so he and Valentin could stay and take part in the theatricals. Sir John then announced that he'd jolly well take a holiday from business too. Everyone seemed happy, natural, animated. Everyone, Mary thought grumpily, except herself.

Valentin did not return, and though Mary lay awake most of the night, Valentin never ventured to her room, either as man or logosh. She was angry with him and did not want to see him. So why did she remain awake in the darkness, listening, hoping to hear his step?

Mary regretted now that she'd run away from Scotland and the family celebrations there. She'd told herself she was tired of all the traditions and festivities, and that a Christmas alone with her son in London would be peaceful and restful.

She now realized that a cheerful family Christmas was exactly what she needed. Meeting Valentin here had brought home to her how much she hated being alone.

Mary wanted Valentin, wanted to be with him in all ways, but Duchess Mina's story had chilled her. Not that she believed Duchess Mina's idea that Valentin lived only for vengeance, but Valentin had hidden so much from her—who knew what else he kept to himself? Mary saw his pain whenever he spoke of Sophie, but he'd never volunteered any information about this tragedy in his life until Mary had pried it from him. She wondered how long he'd have waited before mentioning he'd had a sister at all. If not for Duchess Mina, Mary would never have known.

She slept at long last, and rose, groggy and late for breakfast.

In the sunny morning room, Duchess Mina passed

out the parts for the mummers play and told everyone to work very hard so they could be ready by the next day, which was Christmas Eve. Mary kept herself from snapping a reply that the duchess should have thought to begin preparing long before they came to Hertfordshire.

Mary again bit back irritation when Valentin, looking fresh and rested, strolled into the ballroom where they'd adjourned to rehearse. Mary had been wakeful and uncertain all night, and he looked cool and unruffled, drat him.

The duchess and Julia had decided to improvise a story involving Saint George—sans dragon—a very traditional mummers play. Duke Rudolfo would be Saint George. Sir John would play a dark knight, and he and Rudolfo would battle it out with swords. Saint George would be slain, but a powerful magician, played by Valentin, would bring him back to life.

Julia would be Saint George's intended bride, ready to weep copiously at the death of her beloved. Mary was to play Athena, goddess of wisdom, who came in at the end to drive the sword of justice into the dark knight.

The duchess, as the playwright, decided to narrate and direct. "It is a good way to practice my English," she said. "Mary will make a splendid Athena, will she not, Baron Valentin? So stately in her robes, and she will carry my husband's saber."

Valentin gazed at Mary in silence, and she turned away, unable to meet his eyes.

The rehearsal began. Valentin read out his part in a quiet voice. The only time the play would take Mary near him, it turned out, was at the end, when she would point her sword at Valentin and declare that he was the best of them, because he gave life. That was a mercy at least.

The duchess had them run through the lines and then through the scenes before they broke apart hours later to find appropriate costumes. They would have a rehearsal in costume, Duchess Mina said, and then dinner, as the afternoon was waning. Mary obeyed without argument, too tired to fight Duchess Mina's iron-handed enthusiasm.

Upstairs in her room, Mary donned an ivory-colored evening dress, then instructed her skeptical Scots maid to help drape a sheet around her in classical-looking folds. Mary knotted her hair on top of her head and let a few curls fall to her cheeks. Deciding she looked sufficiently Greek, she made her way to the ambassador's rooms to borrow his saber.

Duke Rudolfo was alone in his sitting room, already strapped into Saint George's makeshift armor. The servants had taken apart several real suits of armor from the main hall and fitted bits of them to the ambassador. The armor looked strange with the swath of white bandage on the duke's shoulder, but Rudolfo had insisted that he was well enough to enact a sword fight—he would use his uninjured arm anyway.

"The English knights must have been uncommonly small," the ambassador complained, adjusting his metal breastplate. "How on earth did they squeeze into this lot? Here is the saber, my dear." Rudolfo lifted a metal sheath from a table and handed it to her, the rings meant to fasten it to a sword belt clinking. "I have put on the tip guard so you do not accidentally skewer Sir John." His eyes twinkled.

Mary lifted the saber and examined the intricately

etched blade. The sword was a thing of beauty, the hilt bearing small and colorful gemstones in a mosaic of abstract design.

"A fine piece of work," Mary said. "I will be careful with it."

"Given to me by the Council of Dukes for my many years of service." Rudolfo looked proud.

"Not a fighting blade, then?" Mary didn't think so — weapons of war tended to be plain and utilitarian. Castle MacDonald was full of war-nicked swords and claymores.

"No, no. It is meant to be worn on formal occasions. But the blade is plenty sharp, so be careful you do not cut yourself."

Mary continued to study the saber, a bright and deadly beauty. "Were you wearing this on the day you went to Baron Valentin's?"

"No, as I said, it was ceremonial …" Rudolfo trailed off, reddening. "Ah, I see what you mean. No, I did not draw it against the Imperial Prince when he went to poor Sophie. It was a dreadful day. I am not happy to think of it."

"Valentin doesn't blame you, you know," Mary said. "Nvengarian politics are so very convoluted and bloody. Or at least they used to be. From what I hear, Prince Damien is trying to stop all that."

Rudolfo looked uncomfortable. "Indeed."

"*I* blame you, though."

Rudolfo jerked his head up, and then he sighed. "What do you want from me, Mrs. Cameron?"

"Me? I want nothing." Mary clenched her hand around the hilt of the sword, the cool metal and smooth gems a contrast to her hot anger. "It is Valentin who hurts. You have never spoken to him of it, have you?"

Rudolfo shook his head. "There is nothing to say."

"An apology if nothing else," Mary said, voice firm. "Valentin lost everything that day, you know. The sister he loved. His position in your society— though I believe he was past caring about that. The Imperial Prince was already a madman from what I understand, uncontrollable. *He* acted as predicted. *You* acted to save your own skin."

"And that of my wife and daughter," Rudolfo said quickly.

"I understand. I might have done the same." Mary paused. "No—I would not have. Dougal, my son, would never forgive me if he knew I'd let a young woman be hurt in order to protect him. He'd expect me to sail in and try to save her. You are Nvengarian—I'm certain you had some sort of weapon handy, even if not this one." She ran her hand along the saber's polished blade.

Rudolfo's face darkened. "You cannot know, my dear. Since that day I have lived with such shame. It eats at me inside. You are quite right—I should have killed the Imperial Prince and faced the consequences. But I feared the retaliation of Grand Duke Alexander against my family as much as I did the Imperial Prince's. One never knows what Alexander will do, even now."

"Your wife seems to think he would have applauded you."

Rudolfo shrugged. "Or made an example of me to show the people of Nvengaria that assassination is discouraged. Even if Alexander himself rejoiced at the death of the Imperial Prince."

Mary lowered the saber. "My brother, Egan, and his wife both speak highly of Grand Duke Alexander. I cannot believe he would be quite so awful to you.

He wanted to rid your land of the horrible man as much as you did."

"And he did, as rumors say." Rudolfo spread his hands. "With poison perhaps. No one knows for certain."

"And then the mad old man's son—Damien— took the throne," Mary said slowly. "I imagine you weren't pleased about that either."

"You English have a saying, eh? That the apple does not fall far from the tree?"

"I am Scottish, and I think the apple fell very far in this case. I've met Damien only briefly, but my brother is his best friend, and Egan could not love a man if he were anything remotely like the old Imperial Prince." Mary gave Rudolfo a decided look. "Egan says Damien is a good man. Valentin believes in Damien as well."

The ambassador frowned, puzzled. "You are wrong about that, my dear. Valentin tried to assassinate Prince Damien. Sneaked into the palace and attacked him with a knife while Damien and his wife sat down to supper. Even now Valentin awaits a chance to topple him from the throne."

Duke Rudolfo spoke with certainty. Was he simply pushing his own desires onto Valentin? Or did Rudolfo believe, with his wife, that Valentin was vengeance-mad?

"Do you truly think you were the intended target, yesterday?" Mary asked. "Not Sir John, as he believes?"

Duke Rudolfo looked surprised. "Of course it was me. Why would someone want to murder your Sir John? He is harmless."

"Yes, he is, really." Mary deflated. "Sir John's wife, my girlhood friend, doted on him."

"It could only have been me they wanted to shoot," Rudolfo said. "I am high in the Council of Dukes, an important man. I imagine all sorts of people wish me dead. Valentin is only one of them."

"I think you should speak to Valentin, Your Grace. Make it right between you."

The ambassador smiled. He was a handsome man when he wasn't trying to be the oily diplomat. "I will try. However, I will insist that I not meet Valentin alone and that I am allowed to stand well beyond reach of his sword when I do."

"I can arrange that. Thank you for lending me your saber, Your Grace. Now I am to go practice my part with Sir John. Your wife says he needs to die more convincingly."

Duke Rudolfo held out his hand. "Thank you, Mrs. Cameron."

He sounded relieved. Mary nodded, relieved as well, as he bowed over her hand, but she couldn't go without a parting shot. "See that you do it."

Mary left the ambassador looking properly chagrined and returned to her chamber to re-pin a drape that had fallen from her shoulder. As she turned from the mirror to snatch up the saber she'd laid on her bed, she glimpsed Sir John walking through the twilit snowy park to the summerhouse at the edge of the garden, near the wood.

"Where is he going?" Mary murmured. She was to have met Sir John in the ballroom.

As Mary peered down from the window, a woman in white, draped similarly to Mary except for a fold of sheet over her head, emerged from the house and hurried after Sir John. A chance beam of the setting sun caught on the sheathed saber the woman carried, very like the one Mary now held.

Mary straightened in shock. Clutching the sword, she hurried to her door and turned the handle. The door refused to budge. Mary shook it, but it was solidly locked.

She was trapped, while outside, Sir John Lincolnbury trotted happily into the summerhouse, followed, he thought, by Mary as Athena, to practice his death scene.

Chapter Nine

VALENTIN KNEW MARY WAS IN DANGER even before he heard her muffled cries. He discarded the velvet robe that was his magician's costume and fled the ballroom where servants were laboring to render it a makeshift theatre.

He realized as he took the stairs two at a time that no one else had sensed what he had. But the logosh in him urged him to find her, protect her ...

When Valentin reached the upper floor, he heard the unmistakable sounds of Mary pounding on her bedchamber door and shouting for help.

He put his hands on the door, his fingers becoming logosh claws. "Mary!"

"Valentin, they've locked me in. Sir John ..."

Valentin let his hands finish becoming demon— his logosh strength was far greater than his human's.

"Stand away," he told Mary. Then he ripped the door from its hinges.

Mary rushed out, swathed like an Athenian

goddess, the ambassador's saber in her hand. Valentin reached for her, but Mary jerked from his grasp, flinging the folds of her draperies to the floor as she ran.

Valentin caught up to her on the stairs. "What has happened? Who did this?"

"She's going to kill him!" was Mary's reply. She dashed the rest of the way down the stairs, and raced through the drawing room and out one of the long French windows.

The evening had clouded over, and a light snow fell from the lowering sky. Mary ran across the park, bare-armed and bareheaded, wearing only dancing slippers. Valentin ran with her, no longer asking questions. He knew with certainty what was about to happen.

As they approached the summerhouse at the end of the garden, Valentin smelled fear overlaid with rage and triumph. And blood.

He growled. He tossed off his coat, the logosh claws tearing away the rest of his clothes. His vision went dark as the beast in him broke through, changing his shape—bone and muscle.

In moments, Valentin stood on four legs, the world now gray and white, its edges slightly curved. His sense of smell became clear—multiple hues and layers of scent radiated from where he stood and flowed across the land.

Mary gazed down at him, wide-eyed, but he knew she didn't fear him. She held up the bare blade, her fingers working something from the saber's tip. She was a warrior, preparing to fight, and Valentin loved her.

Valentin broke down the door of the summerhouse. He dodged back as a bullet screamed past him and buried itself in the doorframe, then he burst all the way in. Mary rushed in right behind him.

Sir John, looking terrified, was slumped on a bench in the octagonal summerhouse, blood smeared on his neck. Duke Rudolfo stood nearby, pistol in hand, acrid smoke hanging in the cold air.

His wife, Duchess Mina, held Valentin's ceremonial sword in both fists. She'd draped herself in a costume like Mary's, and she'd pricked Sir John's throat with the point of the saber. The smell of blood lifted Valentin's lips from his long teeth.

Dimly Valentin reasoned that because the ambassador had fired his shot, his pistol was now empty. Not a threat. But the duchess was armed and could run Sir John through any second. Valentin leapt at her, snarling in animal rage.

The ambassador threw himself between Valentin and his wife. Valentin fell onto Rudolfo, taking him down, Rudolfo's fear filling Valentin's heightened senses.

This was the coward who'd stepped aside when Sophie had been attacked, the man who'd sacrificed Sophie's virtue and sanity to save his own hide.

Valentin hated him. In human form, Valentin could reason that he understood Rudolfo's actions, but the logosh inside him didn't care. This man had let harm come to Valentin's beloved sister, harm that had led to her death.

Valentin wanted to kill. He needed to kill.

Out of the corner of his eye, he saw Duchess Mina raise her saber. The blade came at him, but was met with a clang by Mary's.

Mary shouted something. He saw a sword flash through the air, heard it clatter on the stone floor.

Then the duchess was on the bench next to Sir John. Mary, her dark eyes filled with fury, had her sword's point at Mina's chest.

Under Valentin, the ambassador cried out. Valentin's claws had raked through his clothes to his skin. More blood. *Hot, salty, wet.*

Rudolfo fought, but he was no match for Valentin's strength. *Savage. Kill.*

"Valentin!"

Mary's voice broke through the pounding in Valentin's head. She was afraid, deathly afraid of what he would do to Rudolfo, but she stood straight, her sword unmoving.

"Let him go," Mary said. "Please."

Why? The ambassador was a traitor, a murderer. So was his wife. They should both die.

"Please, Valentin." Mary's voice went soft. "Do not."

The wolf growled in fury, Valentin's need to kill strong. He hadn't forgiven. He wanted blood for blood. It was the way of his people. The cold English did not understand this.

Mary would remind him in her calm voice that she was Scottish. She knew about blood feuds—Highlanders had a long history of them—and yet she was begging Valentin to show mercy.

Mercy. Had Duke Rudolfo shown mercy to Sophie? No, he'd stepped aside and left her to her fate. Rudolfo was as guilty of her suffering and death as the Imperial Prince.

Valentin smelled the guilt now in the ambassador's blood. Guilt, shame, sorrow, fear. Did he deserve mercy?

"Valentin," Mary said again.

He heard the tears in her voice. Mary wanted

Valentin to be the person she thought he was—a good man, a protector. She wanted the guard who'd braved a long journey to lead her sister-in-law, Zarabeth, to safety, the man who'd had compassion enough to forgive Prince Damien for what Damien's father had done.

Mary loved Valentin. She believed in him.

Valentin forced the wolf to leave him. His brain clouded as his limbs stretched and straightened. After what seemed a long time, he found himself panting, on hands and knees on top of the terrified Rudolfo. Rudolfo was flat on his back, his chest a bloody mess, his face pale with dread.

Valentin climbed painfully to his feet. He was naked, his body covered in sweat and blood, but Mary's eyes shone with relief. Sir John looked on, bewildered; the duchess, furious.

"Get up, Rudolfo," Duchess Mina snapped. "Kill him. You must." She gestured at Sir John.

The ambassador shook his head, remaining on the floor, and covered his face with his hands. "No. No more death, my dear. Please."

"Coward! Fool!"

Duchess Mina struggled to rise, but Mary pushed her back with the tip of the saber.

"Stay there, if you please," Mary said coldly. "Consider yourself under arrest. Sir John, go to the house and have someone send for the magistrate. Hurry, please."

Sir John gulped, but under Mary's glare, he climbed to his feet and rushed out.

"We are diplomats," Duchess Mina snarled. Anything innocent and affable about her had vanished. "We do not answer to your magistrate."

"Very well, then you will be asked to leave the

country," Mary returned in a hard voice. "You assaulted Sir John and hired people to shoot him. That is highly illegal in England, I must tell you."

"We will fight you," Mina warned.

"No." Rudolfo sat up, his hand to his bandaged shoulder. "We will return to Nvengaria. We must confess and throw ourselves on the mercy of the Grand Duke."

Duchess Mina gave a shriek of fury. "I will never grovel to Alexander."

"It would be better if you groveled to Prince Damien," Valentin said, his voice gravelly. "*He* might actually listen to you."

"I will never speak to that misery of a prince," the duchess said in disgust. "The offspring of the horror who destroyed Nvengaria? The Imperial Prince's line must cease. It is the only way Nvengaria will be strong."

"Oh, I see." Mary managed to sound calm. "You consider yourself a patriot. Who will rule your country then—your Council of Dukes? I believe Alexander is the head of that, but you do not much like him either, do you?"

"Alexander has finished his usefulness," Duchess Mina said. "Another Grand Duke must take his place and lead Nvengaria to greatness."

Mary turned her cool stare on her. "Let me guess, your husband, Rudolfo?"

"A mad idea." Rudolfo sighed. "It is over, Mina. Please see that."

"Fool," the duchess said, then she went off into a string of Nvengarian. She called her husband, Valentin, Prince Damien, Alexander, and Mary all manner of things. Valentin was glad Mary couldn't understand the filth pouring from her mouth.

The Nvengarian bodyguards burst into the summerhouse, flanked by curious Hertfordshire footmen, eager for a fight. Valentin gave abrupt orders to the bodyguards, who saluted him and moved to take charge of the ambassador and his wife.

Mary at last lowered the sword and stepped away from the duchess. She admonished the guard who bound the duchess's hands to not be cruel, then she walked past Valentin and out into the frigid winter evening.

Valentin went after her, but Mary would not slow or wait for him. Still holding the ambassador's saber, she moved with a quick stride to the lighted house, ignoring the servants who boiled down the garden path past them.

Mary ducked inside through the French door from which they'd exited. In the drawing room the Yule log burned high on the hearth, bathing the chamber in rosy warmth. Mary dropped the saber on a sofa and continued walking.

Julia rushed in from the hall. "Mary, what happened? They will not let me—" She broke off with a squeak when she spotted Valentin standing in the middle of the drawing room, stark naked.

Mary went to her, clapped a hand over Julia's eyes, turned her around, and gave her a shove into the hall. "Go tend to your father, Julia. He was hurt. He will need you."

For once, Julia did not argue. "Yes, Aunt Mary," she said meekly and rushed away.

"Mary," Valentin said.

Mary turned back, body rigid. "Not yet, Valentin. Please."

He folded his arms over his bare chest. "I only

wish to say — thank you for saving me."

Mary nodded once, her eyes a mystery. As she started to turn from him, a new voice filled the outer hall, a light baritone with a Scottish cadence.

"Is that you, Mum? Good Lord, what's all the fracas?"

Joy lit Mary's face. She rushed from the room, and Valentin followed in time to see her fling her arms around a young man who'd entered through the front door.

"Dougal," Mary cried. "Oh, my dear, I am so very happy to see you."

* * *

HUGGING HER SON WAS THE BEST REMEDY in the world, Mary decided. She kissed Dougal's cheek and embraced him again.

"Everything all right, Mum?" Dougal asked, gently pulling back from her. "I've ever seen ye so chuffed to see me before."

Mary pressed her son's face between her hands. She felt the rough of shaved whiskers — good heavens, when had he become such a man? Tall and strong, like Egan. "Nonsense, darling, I am always glad to see you. Goodness, I think you've grown another inch this term."

Dougal was looking past her, brow furrowing. "Did ye know there's a man with no clothes on peering out of th' drawing room? Good Lord, is it Baron Valentin?"

Mary couldn't even blush. "It is."

Dougal laughed. "The pair of ye could be more discreet, ye know. What would Uncle Egan say?"

"Valentin and I are going to be married," Mary said calmly.

"Are ye now?" Dougal sounded much like his

uncle Egan as he looked from Mary to Valentin, who had frozen, his blue gaze hard on Mary. "And ye could nae wait for the wedding night?"

Mary's face heated. "Do not be so silly. This is not …" The feeble words *what it seems* stuck in her throat. "Turn your back so the poor man can go upstairs. We shall speak in the library."

Dougal shrugged good-naturedly and spun to stride through the open door of the library across the hall. Mary gave Valentin a smile, her heart pounding in both fear and joy, before she hurried after Dougal, and Valentin was lost to sight.

* * *

IT WAS NOT UNTIL VERY LATE THAT MARY finally had time to pack her things alone in her chamber. She would leave on the morrow with Sir John, Julia, and Dougal, making for London.

Duke Rudolfo and his wife had been taken to the magistrate's house for the night, under guard of Valentin's trusted men and soldiers from the local regiment. Rudolfo and Mina would begin their return journey to Nvengaria tomorrow. What they'd face there, Mary did not want to imagine.

Dougal explained at the hastily prepared supper the stunned cook gave them that he'd come to Hertfordshire straight from Cambridge. He mourned that he'd arrived too late for the fun when Julia and Sir John told him a breathless tale of events. Mary found that she could not speak of it, and Valentin had disappeared, likely to the magistrate's house with the prisoners.

Mary noted distractedly, as the other three talked, that Julia spoke to Dougal in a friendly, uninhibited way. Julia did not try to preen or be witty; she simply conversed with him as she would an old friend.

Mary found it refreshing, and she could tell Dougal liked Julia in return.

Mary breathed a sigh of relief when she could finally retreat to her room to pack. She jumped only slightly when Valentin opened the door and walked quietly inside.

"Be thankful that I am used to your abrupt comings and goings," she said. "Or I would have screamed."

"You do not scream," Valentin said in a low voice. "Except on special occasions."

His dark tone made her hands shake. "Is all well?" she asked.

Mary expected him to approach her, but Valentin remained heartbreakingly far away. "Duke Rudolfo has fully surrendered to take his punishment. He seems relieved."

"And the duchess?"

Valentin's smile was wry. "Not so relieved. But she knows she will not win."

"She is a regular Lady Macbeth, isn't she?" Mary moved to the dressing table and began folding leather gloves into a box.

"Duchess Mina had many ambitions."

Mary smoothed the gloves, trying to still her fingers. "Funny to think that Sir John was right all along. He *was* the intended target, which is why they enticed him out here in the first place. I recall now what Sir John said when he was introduced to the ambassador at the Hartwells' ball. Remember?" She glanced over her shoulder at Valentin who'd become fixed in the middle of the chamber. "He mentioned all the braid that Nvengarians purchased from England and suggested they were for uniforms. I wondered vaguely why Nvengarians did not have their own braid makers, but I had other things on my mind."

"As did I," Valentin said. "Seeing you erased everything from my thoughts. I paid no attention."

"Well, we ought to have noticed." Mary dropped the gloves into the box and shut the lid, finding it difficult to breathe for some reason. "Duke Rudolfo wanted new uniforms for the army he would raise for the new Nvengaria. But he could not very well order them made in Nvengaria, could he? Sir John did not know why it was important, but they could not risk him inadvertently telling someone who might understand."

No wonder the duchess had been so adamant to draw Julia and Sir John out of London to this house, isolated from the rest of the world. Sir John would be far from his friends, and he might "accidentally" fall through the ice or be hit by a stray shot from a winter shooting party. The country was not always a safe place—hadn't the doctor mentioned a boy who'd been gored by an ox?

"They did not seem to mind so much my knowing," Valentin observed. "They thought I was on their side."

Mary shoved the box of gloves aside in annoyance. "Duchess Mina filled my head with the nonsense that you burned for revenge on her husband. So I would believe you really *did* hire the shooters. She was ready to push the blame onto you if Sir John died. Bloody woman."

Valentin came to her, his face lined and tired. "She was not wrong. I hated Rudolfo, though I would not admit it even to myself. I pretended I had forgiven him, but I secretly hoped I would have to kill him." He cupped Mary's cheek. "You knew that. You stopped me from becoming a murderer."

Mary's eyes stung with unshed tears. "I couldn't bear the thought of you suffering more because of them. I wanted to keep you free. So you could be with me."

Valentin closed the last step between them and gazed down at her. Mary loved his eyes, so deep blue and filled with power, sorrow, and a caring she wanted to reach.

"You told your son we would be married," Valentin said in a quiet voice.

"And I meant it." Mary held his gaze, wishing she could convey what she felt for him. "If you'll have me."

"I told you I have nothing to offer you."

Mary shook her head, her heart lightening as she spoke. "I don't care. I don't want palaces and gold plates and jewels. I have a small house in Edinburgh and rooms of my own at Castle MacDonald. You have your estate in Nvengaria. We will always have a home, and that is all I want. A home. And *you*."

Valentin slid his arm around her waist and caught a tear that fell to her cheek with his thumb. "All I want is *you*, my Mary. I thought that would not be enough for you."

"'Tis more than enough," she whispered. "'Tis riches."

"Mary." Valentin put relief into the word. He nuzzled the line of her hair then moved his warm lips to hers. Mary felt her clothes loosen, his hands on her bare skin. "Enough packing for tonight, I think," he murmured.

"Will you start back to Nvengaria tomorrow?" Mary asked, fearing the answer. "With the ambassador?"

"No." Valentin smiled, his blue eyes warm. "I have resigned. The bodyguards with me were all handpicked by Grand Duke Alexander. They will take the ambassador and his wife back without delay. I have sent a message to Alexander to not expect me with them."

Mary's heart leapt with hope. "Then will you come home with me?"

"To London?"

"No, to Scotland." Her determination swelled. "I have run away long enough. We might miss Christmas Day, but Hogmanay is the bigger celebration anyway."

"I would be pleased to see Castle MacDonald again. It holds for me the happiest memories of my life." Valentin's eyes darkened, and he leaned to kiss the curve of her neck. "Except for my memory of this room, two nights ago."

Mary's pulse sped. "It is a splendid memory for me as well."

"We will make another memory." Valentin feathered kisses down her throat. "One that will last a lifetime."

"I love you," Mary whispered, her heart in her words.

"I love *you*, my Highland Mary." Valentin's eyes danced in sudden amusement. "But perhaps I should not allow you to carry my saber."

Mary sent him a wicked look. "You are absurd. A claymore is much more effective."

Valentin laughed, a rumbling, comforting sound, and she twined her hands behind his neck. "May we begin making those memories now, please?"

"By all means." Valentin swept her into his strong arms and carried her into the bedroom.

"I want to love you all night, Valentin." Mary touched his face as he laid her down, and then his warm weight pressed her into the bed. "And tomorrow, we'll go home."

Epilogue

WHEN THEY REACHED CASTLE MACDONALD several
days later, Mary insisted that Valentin knock on the
door and enter first. Julia and Sir John, a bit
breathless from the precarious ride up the hill to the
castle perched on top, watched, mystified, as
Valentin approached the huge door. Dougal grinned,
knowing why Mary had insisted.

The courtyard was strangely deserted, the castle
quiet. Valentin pounded on the thick door, but only
silence met them when the echoes died away.

Valentin tried the door, found it unlocked, and
pushed it open.

Cheers and laughter erupted from inside the
brightly lit hall. A young Nvengarian woman rushed
forward, her arms outstretched, and the tall, massive
form of Mary's brother followed her. Egan
MacDonald balanced a tiny cloth-wrapped bundle in
his great hand.

"Welcome, First-Footer!" the young woman cried,

hugging Valentin. "Remember, Valentin, you were to have been our first-footer last year? And then …"

"I got shot," Valentin said, warmth touching him. He'd been left to die out in the cold, but Egan had found and rescued him. Then Mary had come to Valentin's chamber to nurse him, finding him bare in his bed …

"I have brought your sister," Valentin said to Egan. He drew Mary into the circle of his arm. "And Dougal. And friends."

The Highlanders inside—Mary's cousins and their neighbors, the Rosses, cheered again. Cousin Angus shouted, "More friends, more whisky!"

Mary held out her arms for Egan's bundle. Egan relinquished it carefully, and Mary peeled back a blanket to gaze at the next heir to Castle MacDonald.

Charlie Olaf MacDonald had been born not long before Mary had departed. Mary marveled at how much he'd grown in the scant weeks she'd been gone. She remembered wanting to escape the collective joy of the house, a joy she'd not felt part of.

She realized how foolish she'd been. Of course she was part of the happiness, and now she could bring Valentin into it with her.

Mary handed the baby to Zarabeth, who hugged Charlie to her as though he were the most precious thing on earth.

"There will be more celebrations at Hogmanay," Mary said to her merry family and friends. "I have asked Valentin to be my husband."

Valentin, behind her, enfolded Mary in his arms and drew her back against him. "And I have accepted."

Egan let out a roaring laugh. "That's my sister. Never a demure, soft-spoken creature was she! As laird, let me be the first to say — Welcome to the family. If ye can stand us, that is."

The MacDonald clan behind him yelled at this and pelted Egan with bits of mistletoe. Valentin rested his cheek against Mary's hair, his unshaved whiskers pleasantly rough. "I believe I will be able to stand it," he said. Mary turned and met his lips with hers.

"Aye, and there is nae even mistletoe above them," Dougal said in mock disgust.

To the sound of more cheers, Egan and Zarabeth led them all into the Great Hall, Valentin with his arm around Mary.

Everything was as Mary remembered, the high beams, the huge hearth, the sense of light and happiness. The long tables were laden with food, and fiddlers and drummers waited in the corner. As the family filed into the hall, the musicians struck up a lively tune.

Dougal seized Julia's hands and danced her into the center of the room. Men and women paired up, and a flame-haired, buxom MacDonald woman grabbed Sir John to be her partner.

Mary clasped Valentin's hands and spun around and around with him as the fiddlers played and the drummers beat a rapid time. Mary was a Highland woman, and this music was in her blood, as was her fighting spirit. She'd no longer be afraid to leave these shores and travel to far-off Nvengaria, because she understood now that friends awaited her there too.

But it would be inevitable that she and Valentin would come back here — always. Mary was a part of Scotland as much as Valentin was a part of Nvengaria. And no matter where she and Valentin

roamed, it would always be home where they were—
together.

Valentin pulled Mary into his arms and held her
close as the Highlanders danced around them. Julia
was flushed with happiness, and Sir John attempted
a mad jig that had everyone hooting with laughter.

"Sophie would have loved this," Valentin said as
he and Mary withdrew into a corner.

"My darling, I am so sorry that I never got to meet
her," Mary said, hurting for him.

Valentin nodded. Sorrow filled his eyes, but the
anguish, the stark grief, had faded. "You would have
loved her as I did. But she is with me again, in my
heart. When you stopped me from killing the
ambassador, she returned to me." Valentin touched
his chest. "She is happy for us."

Mary did not know whether he spoke
metaphorically or whether Nvengarian magic really
did allow him to know what Sophie felt. It did not
matter, she realized. Valentin had found his peace.

Mary leaned against his tall strength. "Welcome
home, my love." She gestured at the Highlanders
spinning to the music. "To all the family you can
handle."

"I believe I can handle you best of all," Valentin
murmured. He licked the shell of her ear. "I look
forward to bed."

"We had better wait, I think, unless you want
them all following us upstairs and shouting lewd
remarks outside the door."

Valentin looked surprised but not alarmed. "I am
happy to dance with you for now. Tonight, we will
begin the rituals of Nvengarian courtship."

"Rituals?" Mary raised her brows. "What sort of
rituals?"

Valentin's blue eyes, with their slightly inhuman cast, darkened with promise. "They are numerous, and very erotic."

Pleasant heat snaked through Mary's body. "I anticipate them with much interest."

"That is my brave, Highland lass."

Mary kissed him again, ignoring the whoops from around the room as the kiss turned passionate. Valentin traced Mary's cheek, took her hands, and pulled her back into the dance.

End

Author's Note

I hope you enjoyed Mary and Valentin's story! It was originally printed in an anthology called *A Christmas Ball*, and I'm happy to be able to present it on its own.

When I first accepted the request to contribute a story to *A Christmas Ball*, I was under severe word-count restriction—I remember going through and taking out so many things! In this version I was able to restore what I'd been forced to cut or expand scenes I thought had been given short shrift.

I have enjoyed re-releasing the four tales of the Nvengarian series (*Penelope and Prince Charming; The Mad, Bad Duke; Highlander Ever After; The Longest Night*). I have great fondness for this mixed world of historical and fantasy, with its fairy-tale kingdom where all kinds of magic can happen.

Thanks again for joining me in these stories about the fairy-tale kingdom of Nvengaria and its wild inhabitants.

Keep reading for a look at one of my other re-

releases, *The Pirate Next Door*, a tale of what happens when a pirate moves in next door to a proper widow in Regency London.

All my best,

Jennifer Ashley

Please turn the page
for a preview
of

*The
Pirate
Next Door*

Regency Pirates
Book 1

Chapter One

London, June, 1810

ALEXANDRA ALASTAIR LAY IN HER SLIM-POSTED BED beneath green silk hangings, her hands flat on the coverlet, and debated whether she dared add the viscount next door to her list of eligible suitors.

Grayson Finley, Viscount Stoke.

She knew very little about him, save that he'd disappeared from England as a lad and had turned up again a week ago to take the title of Viscount Stoke, left to him by his second cousin.

Alexandra's friend Lady Featherstone had discovered that the new viscount was thirty-five years of age, unmarried, and quite rich. Very possibly, Lady Featherstone had speculated, he'd opened up the house in Grosvenor Street because he intended to seek a wife.

He certainly was different from the other gentlemen on Alexandra's list, who were all polite, respectable, and likely to make her a quiet and steadfast second husband. Her first husband had been anything but steadfast, dying by falling down the stairs in the house of one of his mistresses.

Alexandra's head throbbed in the summer night's humid air. Thoughts of her deceased husband always made her head ache. Which was why she and Lady Featherstone had so carefully pared down the list, learning about any shortcomings of each gentleman on it. The gentlemen who had succeeded in remaining on the list were dependable, trustworthy, respectable.

And dull. Hopelessly dull. Alexandra squeezed her eyes shut.

The viscount, on the other hand, was extremely interesting. His skin was sun-bronzed, a liquid color that spoke of lands far from foggy London, and he wore his gold-streaked hair unfashionably long and pulled into a queue. His gaze, which lingered on Alexandra more than was polite when they passed at their front doors, showed her that his eyes were dark blue like twilight in June.

Sometimes he went out with only a loose greatcoat shrugged on over a shirt and calfskin breeches, and leather boots that reached above his knees. His broad shoulders filled out his coat, and the small smile he sent her way made Alexandra's heart race.

Yes, he was quite different. Alexandra refused to let herself use Lady Featherstone's words — *most splendidly and magnificently handsome.*

The carriages and horses the viscount hired were fine, but Annie and Amy, her twin downstairs maids, had told her that he'd opened up only a few rooms in the house next door. Everything else remained dark, dusty, and unused.

The viscount kept a massive manservant with very dark skin and a bald head creased with scars. Alexandra's footman, Jeffrey, a big lad, was terrified of the viscount's manservant. Of course, it was difficult to imagine someone of whom Jeffrey was *not* terrified.

Other gentlemen who came and went included a young man of about her own age, who dressed as casually as the viscount, and a short man with a leathery face, a cheerful grin, and an Irish brogue.

None of them looked terribly steady and dependable. But, on the other hand, definitely not dull.

Alexandra opened her eyes and took a long breath, trying to still the pounding in her head. She wanted a steady and dependable gentleman, did she not? One who, above all, had a fondness for children. Because if she did not marry one of the steady and dependable gentlemen from the list, Alexandra Alastair would never have children.

Once, long ago, she'd borne a child. Her husband had looked almost relieved when the little lad had died, only hours old. Alexandra's grief had taken her to a place of darkness, from which she'd never quite returned. Theophile had pretty much ignored her after that, and Alexandra had never conceived again.

A cooling breeze from the window touched the tears on her cheeks. Her bedchamber faced her garden, and the scent of new roses drifted to her from the vines at the windows. She loved her garden, which had been her retreat, her sanctuary, during her five years of marriage to Theophile Alastair.

From the garden now, she heard voices. Male voices.

They came to her quite clearly — sharp, angry, grim. Puzzled, Alexandra brushed the tears from her cheeks and sat up.

She realized that the voices came not from her garden but from the house next door. The window next to hers must be open, and sounds were floating from one house to the next.

Alexandra flipped back the covers and slid from the bed, her feet finding the warmth of her slippers. She snatched up the peignoir that lay on the armchair and slid it on, tying the ribbons down the front. She approached the window and pulled back the drape.

A man's voice, drawling and unfamiliar, was saying, "So tell me, Finley, why a man from the Admiralty visited you today. If I like your answer, I might just let you live."

* * *

GRAYSON FINLEY STRUGGLED FOR BREATH. The coarse rope cut his throat as his feet scrabbled for purchase, and more rope burned his wrists behind his back.

The dim, dry part of his mind reflected that he'd survived James Ardmore's near-hanging trick before. That time, Ardmore had relented and cut him down, but only after he'd extracted a terrible promise. This time . . . who the hell knew what Ardmore had in mind this time?

Grayson's toes would not quite take his weight, only enough to keep the noose from completely cutting off his breath. Ardmore had looped the rope through a heavy ring in the ceiling, and he held the other end, able to pull the rope tight or loosen it as he chose. Ardmore wanted Grayson to struggle, to *almost* succeed in saving himself, until Grayson grew too tired of fighting and dropped, crushing his own throat.

The dark-haired, grim-faced Ardmore had once been Grayson's closest friend. Grayson had rescued Ardmore from a cage on a pirate ship, and later, the two had joined the mutiny that had launched the adventures of Ardmore and Finley, co-captains of the *Majesty* and the terror of the seas. They'd been all of eighteen years old.

Ardmore had burst in not an hour before with his band of pirate hunters. Jacobs, Grayson's second-in-command, had held them off while Grayson got Maggie to safety. Jacobs was lying downstairs now, holding his wounded side, five of Ardmore's men pointing pistols at him. They'd trussed up Grayson and hauled him upstairs so Ardmore could string him up and try to learn his secrets.

He jerked on the rope, and Grayson's feet left the ground. Black danced before his eyes. Ardmore drawled in his Charleston accent, "*Tell me.* Or Jacobs dies."

Grayson drew stinging air into his throat. He didn't really give a damn whether Ardmore found out English secrets, and throwing Ardmore a bone might make the man leave him alone for a while. "The French king."

Ardmore's eyes narrowed. "The last French king was beheaded twenty years ago."

"King in exile. Gone missing."

The rope slackened. Grayson's feet hit the floor. He gulped air, fire flickering the edges of his vision.

"Louis Bourbon?" Ardmore asked in genuine surprise. "The English have lost track of their pet monarch? Interesting. What do they expect *you* to do about it?"

"They think pirates in pay of French agents took him," Grayson said the best he could. "They think I'll know who's capable of smuggling him back to France. Besides you, I mean."

"So they have you hopping to find out where he is? Or, what, they'll arrest you for past crimes?"

"Something like that."

Ardmore seemed to think this amusing, then he gave Grayson a long, cold look. He tied the rope fast to the bedpost, the line taut enough so that Grayson's toes just touched the floor if he stretched them. Ardmore had been tying lines for seventeen years, and Grayson knew the knot would not be weak.

"I'll leave you now," Ardmore said. "Maybe Oliver will return in time to save you. Maybe he won't. In the meantime, you can hang there and wonder how long it will take for you to die."

Grayson tried to swallow air, tried to lean his head back to open his throat. Ardmore came close to Grayson and looked up into his face. "It took my brother a long time to die," he said. "Think on that while you dance."

His light green eyes were like ice. The trouble between Captains Ardmore and Finley had started on a long-ago day when Grayson had married the Tahitian woman, Sara, whom Ardmore had loved. That event had led, across years and through the waterways of the world, to James Ardmore staring up at Grayson in this London bedchamber and wishing him dead.

Ardmore gave Grayson a final look of cold fury and left the room, his heavy footsteps ringing in the hall. Grayson heard him descend the staircase then give curt orders to his men below. The front door opened, and, after a moment, closed. Then, silence.

The rope creaked from the ring in the ceiling. The ring also supported the chandelier, an iron thing from centuries past. If Grayson jerked hard enough, he might dislodge the circle of iron, which could sever the rope. Or, the chandelier might fall and crush the life out of him.

The bed was too far across the room to be of any use, but the straight-backed chair might help. Now to discover if Ardmore had left it just out of reach or near enough.

As Grayson walked his toes toward the chair, he damned himself for lowering his guard. Ardmore and his men had overwhelmed him and Jacobs while they'd supped alone together, trying to figure out how they were going to find Louis Bourbon for the Admiralty and gain pardon for Grayson's acts of piracy. He'd wondered why Ian O'Malley, Ardmore's man sent to watch Grayson, had gone out and not returned. Grayson should have been more suspicious.

Grayson's foot reached the chair. He managed to hook his straining toes around its leg and jerk it toward him. His foot slipped, and he lost hold of the chair and swung heavily against the rope. His vision went black.

He heard voices from the stairs, ones he didn't know, and a feminine cry. Pattering footsteps filled the room, accompanied by the rustling of silk and a brush of scent. Slim arms wrapped his legs and tried to lift him.

"Help me," the female voice said. "Jeffrey, quickly, cut him down."

Another pair of arms, heavier and stronger, caught Grayson's hips and hoisted him upward. The rope went slack around Grayson's throat, and he dragged in gulps of air, fire dancing behind his eyes.

"I don't have a knife, madam," a boyish voice said.

A gruff woman answered him. "Take this one."

Grayson's vision began to clear. He heard the chair skitter on the floor, then the frame creak as a large lad clambered upon it. The young man lifted his arms, bathing Grayson in the smell of unwashed body. The lad sawed through the rope with the knife, his sinewy hands working quickly.

The rope broke, and Grayson fell. His legs buckled, and he landed flat on his face on the carpet.

A scent as sweet as summer sunshine washed over him, and a light hand touched his shoulder. "Jeffrey, run after them. Fetch a watchman."

"But they're murderers, madam," the lad bleated. "I'm afraid of murderers."

Grayson stifled a laugh and dragged in breath after breath, inhaling the stale smell of the carpet mixed with her heady perfume.

A cool blade touched his wrist, and the ropes loosened. Free, his hands landed at his sides, burning as the blood flowed back to them. He lay still, enjoying his pain, because pain meant life.

His next-door neighbor knelt over him, her pretty eyes anxious as she touched his shoulder. He'd spied the woman a few times in passing since he'd moved in and had found her worth a second glance. And worth deliberately inventing a reason to be leaving his house whenever he saw her carriage depositing her at her front door.

He'd ordered Jacobs to find out who she was. His lieutenant had reported that she was a widow called Mrs. Alastair, and before that, Miss Alexandra

Simmington, daughter of Lord Alexis Simmington, the second son of a duke.

Blue blooded and well bred. And his rescuer.

Grayson was in love. Red-brown hair fell in a riot of curls over her shoulders, and her eyes were brown, flecked with green, like the waters of a woodland pond. She wore a feminine and frilly garment of green silk that clung to nicely rounded curves. If he slid open the bows on the front of the gown, it would part and show him the glories of her inside.

She rubbed his wrists without compunction, pushing the blood back through them. His hands stung, hot needles in his flesh.

Grayson wanted to thank her, but words would not come from his nearly crushed throat. He rolled himself onto his back, drawing in the air that Ardmore's rope had denied him.

She was speaking. "We found another man downstairs, hurt. I think he'll be all right, but he needs attending."

He heard her without understanding, the words flowing over his tired body and giving him strength. More strength would come if he touched her. He slid his aching hands to her waist, and her warm, slippery gown welcomed him, her curves supple beneath it.

Wordless desire welled up in him, spun by the nearness of death and the nearness of *her*. Grayson pulled her closer. Her eyes flickered in nervousness, her long lashes sweeping to hide them.

Her face was finely curved, flesh sculpted to bone, a small scattering of freckles dusting her nose. Her chin was a tiny bit plump, and her lips were shell pink, not reddened by artifice.

Without a conscious decision to do so, Grayson lifted his head and brushed a kiss to her mouth.

She pulled back, but not in anger, a modest young woman. Her red-brown brows drew together as she studied him, as though he were a specimen for a scientific paper.

Grayson slid his hand to the nape of her neck, kneading softly, gentling his touch. She relaxed, just a little, and Grayson kissed her again, this time more firmly. After a moment, pretty Mrs. Alastair gave a little sigh, and he felt a small, answering push of lips.

Excitement, uncontrolled and uncaring, washed through him. He suddenly wanted her, this lovely, sweet-smelling woman who'd lifted him from death. His kiss became more forceful. She made a soft noise of surprise, but Grayson's body took over.

He opened her mouth with his tongue, and satisfyingly, she did not fight him. She fitted her mouth to his, but clumsily, as though she were unused to opening for a man, unused to accepting such a deep kiss. Her lips warmed as she let herself learn.

Grayson broke the kiss, but only to roll her over, to take her to the floor beneath him. The lacy garment was no barrier between himself and her warm curves, and her breasts pressed unashamedly against his chest. He slanted his mouth across hers again, kissing her swollen lips, scooping up the goodness of her onto his tongue.

She made another small noise — of surrender or protest, he couldn't tell. He was stiff with longing, harder than he'd been in a long time. Grayson pressed her thighs apart, molding the thin garment to her, feeling the heat of her through the silk. His fingers fumbled at the little bows, wanting to part the garment and have at her.

A strong hand landed on his shoulder. "That will be enough of *that*, my lord," a woman said.

Darkness receded, and Grayson jerked back to the present. He'd forgotten the coarse-voiced woman and the beefy, terrified youth who'd accompanied his rescuer. Grayson raised his head to find the two of them staring down at him while he lay on top of their mistress, the large woman scowling, the lad openmouthed in fascination.

Grayson rolled away from Mrs. Alastair's ripe, sweet body and curled his arms over his stomach. He drew in a breath of sweet air, and with it came laughter. He laughed for the joy of life and the joy of the beautiful woman on the carpet beside him.

She sat up and stared at him in bewilderment. He lifted his hand and touched the curve of her face.

"Thank you," he whispered. "My rescuer."

* * *

Grayson Finley, Viscount Stoke, seemed a very resilient man. Alexandra watched the animation flow back into his body, like water returning to a dry pool, when only a moment ago he'd lain still, content to simply be alive.

After only a few more minutes flat on his back, he climbed to his feet, looking as energetic as a man who'd just risen from a refreshing sleep. His throat was dark with bruises, but other than that, he seemed little worse for wear.

Blue eyes sparkling, he ordered the quaking Jeffrey and Cook downstairs to find the man called Mr. Jacobs. To Alexandra, he said, "Come with me."

No explanation, no waiting, not even dressing himself, for heaven's sake. He wore leather breeches, a linen shirt opened to his waist, and tall boots. No collar, no waistcoat, no coat. A white scar ran from the hollow of his throat to disappear into the shadow of muscle under the shirt. Alexandra found herself wanting to tilt her head to trace the path of the scar to its end.

His nose was crooked, as if it had been broken, and another scar pulled his lower lip downward at the left corner. Not necessarily a perfect face, but an arresting one all the same.

The candlelight in the hall glinted on his sun-streaked hair and shone faintly on gold bristles of new beard. Alexandra's late husband had never allowed his beard to appear. The moment Theophile spotted a whisker, he'd shout for his valet to, for God's sake, come and remove it. He'd wanted his face perpetually smooth and clean. Alexandra had heard rumors that he liked his women just as bare in certain places, but she'd never been brave enough to find out if this were true.

The viscount took her hand to pull her up the next flight of stairs. His palm was callused and hard, very unlike the soft, manicured hands of the cultured gentlemen on her list. The leather of his scarred boots bent and flowed around his joints with the ease of long use.

Despite the candles, the house was dark, the paneling that lined the walls nearly black. The stairs held the patina of age and creaked under the viscount's tread. Alexandra glimpsed rooms through open doors where dust sheets had been removed from the furniture, but in others, chairs and tables were still draped in cloth. Crates stood about, some opened, some tightly shut.

They entered a bedchamber on the top floor, which, Alexandra calculated, lay just on the other side of the third floor rooms in her house. This room had not been opened — the dust sheets remained on what little furniture filled it, and the fireplace was long cold.

The viscount strode unerringly to a panel that looked like any other panel in the dark wall and touched a piece of raised molding. The paneling swung away to reveal a small, square compartment.

From this niche, to Alexandra's amazement, sprang a girl.

She was about twelve years old and dressed in a soiled pink silk gown with many ruffles and bows, most of them torn. In her right hand, the girl held a long and wicked-looking knife. She swept her midnight black hair from her face, revealing sparkling dark eyes under black slanted brows.

"Papa!" she cried. She flung her arms about the viscount's waist, dagger and all. "I was so frightened Captain Ardmore would kill you. Are you all right?"

End of Excerpt

About the Author

New York Times bestselling and award-winning author Jennifer Ashley has written more than 75 published novels and novellas in romance, urban fantasy, and mystery under the names Jennifer Ashley, Allyson James, and Ashley Gardner. Her books have been nominated for and won Romance Writers of America's RITA (given for the best romance novels and novellas of the year), several *RT BookReviews* Reviewers Choice awards (including Best Urban Fantasy, Best Historical Mystery, and Career Achievement in Historical Romance), and Prism awards for her paranormal romances. Jennifer's books have been translated into more than a dozen languages and have earned starred reviews in *Booklist*.

More about Jennifer's series can be found at http://www.jenniferashley.com. Or join her newsletter at http://eepurl.com/47kLL

CPSIA information can be obtained
at www.ICGtesting.com
Printed in the USA
LVOW11s1631120117
520748LV00004B/913/P